Friends, Foes & the 5%

RON KRIT

Thank you to my editors, friends, and family.
I appreciate all the people that listened
to me endlessly talk about my books.

Special thanks to my boys. This is for you.

MARCH MADNESS

In a friendly, almost brotherly tone, Sam stares at Jay (aka Coop) and yells, "Stop being a little bitch! You need to enter this contest. Really. Fifty K. Stop taking my cash and make some real money."

Gambling is nothing new to Coop. He takes everyone's money, but nothing over a few grand.

"Sam, I only want your money. It's Saturday night and I think you need to get laid."

"I've been single for thirty seconds. I just need to get drunk."

"That is loser talk. I'm the best wingman ever. I should've been a pilot."

Sam shakes his head in disapproval. "I will never understand how someone with such a horrible sense of humor and low level of attractiveness meets so many women. Then again, you also graduated with honors and never went to class." Sam has always been jealous of Coop. And if he's not going to put some money on college basketball, Sam will do it for him. Sam rationalizes stealing Jay's basketball picks by offering him the cash if he wins.

The bar down the street from Coop's place is packed full of recent college grads. You can tell because everyone is drinking beer or cheap shots. Young women make Sam uncomfortable, even though he and Coop are in a similar age bracket.

With a sincere gaze, "I know you liked Julie. She sucked. Drink this shot, relax, and let's just enjoy ourselves." Coop's ability to say the right thing is what should've landed him in sales, but instead he's a day trader. He sits at his slightly messy desk, with piles of research, and always seems to eke out a decent paycheck, completely ignoring that research.

"I am puzzled, Coop. Why do you have Nina do research for you? It seems that you never actually read all that paperwork."

"Sammy, baby, it's an emotional market. And when things are not moving in one direction or another because of emotions, I use the research. Stop thinking." A few more drinks come their way and a slight buzz sets in. Not that he's an alcoholic, but Coop is most relaxed either when he's buzzed or running.

A blond who spent a little too much time in the sun sits next to Sam. Before she can order a water, Coop grabs a glass from the bar and a water pitcher, and hands her a drink. She smiles, "How did you know?"

Coop shouts at the bartender, "Three shots of Patron."

"I'm Jay Cooper. Call me Coop. This is Sam. Call him Sammy." The shots come faster than expected. Coop whispers in Sam's ear, "Be quiet and offer to walk her home. She's tired and horny."

"I'm Shelly. I'm going to ignore the fact you gave me water because of the horrible tan/red lines on my face. No idea the sun was going to burn me. It was fifty today. That's how you know I'm a real blonde."

Sammy follows orders well. Coop has introduced him to more women since they met in college than he ever thought existed. With an innocent smile, "I think the moonlight has burned me before."

Sam and Shelly exchange smiles as Coop excuses himself. Looking back at the couple, Coop is proud. An image whizzes through his head—a wedding invitation ... Sam Linch and Shelly. He can't make out anything else.

Pushing his way back to them through the crowd, "One more shot, something a little odd, so we never forget it." Shelly loves the thought of this; Sam hates when Coop does this.

"Okay, Coop. Another toast," Coop holds up his hand to silence his buddy, "To Shelly Belly!"

Jay Cooper does not have a death wish, but he believes his life will end on the young side. His fear of death and ability to see the future make him force moments. If Coop said the truth—this is your future wife—it would have ruined everything. It always does.

The last drink goes down easy and feels good. Coop looks for someone who will enjoy his witty banter. It's actually better that way. It ruins the fun when you know right off the bat which girl will sleep with you.

Most women find Coop charismatic. With his eminent death wish, he lives life with a lot of gusto.

As Sammy loves blondes, Coop drifts towards brunettes. Coop's eyes are slightly closed; it's what he does when he's had too much to drink. Usually, Sam would get him water because he knows how much Coop hates to get too drunk. However, Sam has already left, and Coop is celebrating a future wedding. He has no idea that this lady has been watching him since he walked in the door.

"Hi handsome." Coop attempts to open his eyes wide, trying to focus and show he's being sincere.

"Aren't you forward? I like that in a woman." All she wants to be told is how beautiful she is. "I have to return the compliment. You have this amazing," pausing for what seems like a little too long, "everything."

"Natalie, and thank you." Coop's warm hand kisses her tanned shoulder. Natalie smiles again, and Coop melts. He's a sucker for a nice smile.

"That smile, this is going to come out odd, but it reminds me of my mom." Water forms in his eyes, not enough for a tear but it's noticeable and comforting. The music in the bar is loud and chatter makes it impossible to hold a conversation. And Coop senses Natalie wants to talk.

Natalie is surprisingly okay being compared to a stranger's mom. "That's sweet."

A stumbling Coop grabs a bottle of water as Natalie walks away. A moment, an explosion of energy and butterflies hit as Natalie walks away. Confusion flushes over him. Was the image he saw earlier his wedding reply card or Sammy's wedding invitation? Feeling self-assured that he dies alone, he tries to enjoy the moment. Coop calls out, "Natalie, wait."

"Can I get your number?" Reaching into her tiny red purse, Natalie pulls out a business card. Too drunk to read the company, he takes the card and gives her a hug. She kisses him on the cheek.

Her soft lips push against Coop for what seems like a week. Her breasts are pressed into his chest, and his hands sit on the top of her jeans. Her arms squeeze him tightly, as if she knows how much he loves to be hugged like that.

The moment ends and she takes his warm hand and interlocks it with her cold hand. Coop asks, "Are you using me for my body heat?"

She laughs and shakes her head no. Coop remarks, "Listen, I'm okay with that. Use me."

Before Coop can offer up a walk home, or some late-night tacos, Natalie hops in a cab. Not afraid to drink alone, Coop heads back to the bar.

"Water and whiskey," he says. Then, to clarify for the confused-looking bartender, "A glass of each. Thanks."

FAMILY BONDING

Sunday morning slowly fills sun into Coop's apartment. Shelly is trying to figure out how the coffee maker works as Coop tries to piece back the night. Part of his amazing brain does not allow him to forget much. It's like he took notes:

- *Help Sam meet Shelly*
- *Natalie approaches him*
- *She was watching him*
- *Great boobs*
- *Phone number*
- *Whiskey*
- *Pass out*
- *She figures out coffee maker*

"What are you doing here, Shelly?"

"Well, I failed at trying not to wake you. Sammy's coffee machine is broken. He said you wouldn't mind. That, and you sleep like a baby on Sunday mornings."

Shaking his head in agreement, "Not at all. Sammy never has coffee. He thinks I'm his personal Starbucks. Really, every morning he grabs a cup before leaving for work. And an egg sandwich."

Before her coffee is done, Coop hops out of bed in sweatpants and a shirt that reads, "I have a black belt in keeping it real." Shelly looks puzzled as Coop puts two pieces of toast in the toaster and starts the frying pan.

Coop magically reads her mind, "So you want mushrooms, cheese and spinach. Sammy will eat that, too."

"You are an odd man, Coop, but I like you. How did you know mushrooms, cheese and spinach?"

"That's like the official, I have a vagina omelet." Sharing a laugh, Jay makes the eggs and calls Sammy. "Get your lazy ass down here. I cannot believe you would send your girl to get you coffee and breakfast. A stranger, for real? What's a matter with you? Have you seen the guns on your friend?"

Sammy sincerely apologizes. "Sorry, buddy. I thought you would be asleep. You normally take Sundays off."

Firing back quickly, "From the gym, not life, asshole. Come down here for breakfast. And bring me some corned beef."

With a raised eyebrow, Shelly playfully says, "You guys have an odd relationship. And how are you okay with people just barging into your apartment for coffee?"

"Good point. I'll get an alarm system, and a dog. And when I'm hungover, I crave salt."

As the eggs cook, Jay explains the pictures hanging on the walls; they were painted by his mother. The four file cabinets are full of research his partner, Nina, does, and the couch is much more comfortable than the bed. Sensing further curiosity in his guest, "Go ahead, check out the bedroom and bathroom. "

"It's much cleaner in here than I anticipated." With no hesitation, Shelly takes inventory, not like a robber or a furniture snob, but like an innocent child. "Love the record player. You're an old soul, Coop."

Sammy finally interrupts his best friend and possible girlfriend's awkward jibber jabber. "Sorry, Coop. I needed to do some cleaning. It's been a while since I had a girl over."

"How many times do I need to tell you Sammy? Clean your bathroom all the time. Buy more than corned beef, peanut butter and jelly, wheat bread, and orange juice. Am I charging you too much in rent?"

Laughing, "I can afford food. I thought breakfast was our thing."

Shelly is thoroughly impressed with Coop's place. "Don't be impressed. I work out of here. I have a coworker come over a few times a week. It must be clean. Now eat your eggs, and don't forget to tip your server."

The post-hangover headache kicks in as Sammy and Shelly start to eat. Coop takes two slices of corned beef and tosses them in the frying pan with an egg. "Quit judging me. What kind of woman breaks into a stranger's apartment? You are one trusting girl."

Scarfing down her sandwich quicker than Sammy embarrasses her, she ignores the feeling and presses Jay. "Listen, Coop, you know what girls want in their omelet; I know a semi-decent man when I meet him. And that was delicious."

"Compliments taken. Now get out of here. Remember, I take Sundays off."

There is something different about Shelly. She actually cares about people. Before Sammy can ask for more coffee, it's poured, and she put all the dishes in the dishwasher. Sammy deserves a nice girl; maybe this will work like Coop pictured last night. "Stop cleaning up; although uninvited, you are still a guest. Besides, Sammy's place needs a cleaning way more than mine."

Walking slowly upstairs, Shelly turns to Sammy and stares at him with sweet green eyes and says, "I like him. Don't think I'm a snooper, but he has a box with lots of trophies sticking out of it. Is he some sort of athlete?"

Shaking his head because everyone asks Sam questions about Coop, "He's too humble to put them out." Today, Sam is okay with sharing Coop info because unlike most nights, he woke up with a wonderful girl.

"Everyone asks about the box. I told him months ago to either put them up somewhere or toss them. His mother was so proud of them, but he thinks it's too braggadocious. He has trophies for martial arts and baseball. I think he won Golden Gloves when we were in college, but I can't remember."

Surprised, "I cannot see him fighting."

"You don't want to. I only saw him get in one or two fights. Visiting friends in Austin, some muscle head was upset that Coop was talking to his girl. It happened so fast. The giant grabbed his girlfriend by her wrist. Not in a sweet way, and I've never seen Coop so mad. It was like he knew the dude beat her. Coop said something like, 'Come on, WWE, no need to hurt your girl.' The macho man said, 'Maybe I'll just hurt you.' This was all like a bad rom-com movie. And as this dude's massive hand reaches for Coop, he grabs it and drags the guy into his knee. Grossest thing I've ever seen. A few teeth popped out and we ran."

Shelly comments, "Nasty," and promptly switches subjects. "Can we take a bath?"

Sammy is a little bit taken aback. Not many women are this open. Then again, they already had sex, so why not.

The running water from the bath sounds like a rain shower in Coop's apartment. The sound relaxes him. Instead of waiting the standard two days, he calls Natalie.

Her sultry voice greets him with excitement, "HELLO!"

"Hi, Natalie. It's your boyfriend."

"Hm. Michael, Bobby, David? Something Cooper."

With a smile, "There you go. Call me Coop." Immediately Coop feels at ease.

Natalie's interest in Coop started a week ago when she saw him at the bar. His smile and warmth felt real. Although she hunted him, she plays coy, "You couldn't wait another day to call me, could you?"

Trying not to read her thoughts Coop senses something is off. His paranoia that the phone is tapped forces him to keep his cool. "How about coffee?"

"Coop, I thought you would never ask. How about Lovely, on Milwaukee? Eleven?"

Excited, Coop fires back, "Perfect. I'll be the one wearing a pink carnation."

THE FIVE PERCENT

Distrust, which forms often in Coop's head, becomes anger. Natalie must be recruiting him. Fuck. Drinking always dulls his senses; an agent was bound to find him. Why did she have to be so hot?

Natalie arrives at the bakery in style. She's wearing an old school rugby shirt, Yankees hat, and black shorts that reveal long, toned legs. Her sweet hug continues to confuse Coop.

Coop cuts to the chase. "Impressive, you knew I liked donuts and took my coffee with two sugars. Your gift is much stronger than mine."

With no smile, Coop cuts to the chase, "Why me? Who do you work for?"

Sensing his angst, "Coop, I want a friend. I want someone who understands what it's like to know things. I knew the moment I saw you a week ago, you were in the five percent. I just ran away from New York and needed to make sure you didn't work for the government—or worse, the mob. I felt that I could trust you. And that line about your mom, it was sweet." Staring into her magically blue eyes, Jay knows she's telling the truth but hiding something.

Trying to have some compassion, "The five percent are gamblers, mobsters, cheats, and then there are the ones trying to be superheroes. Which one are you?"

Tears form deep in the corner of her eyes, "I left a job working on Wall Street because the CIA targeted me. They wanted to know if my boss was a crook. She was not a crook, but I ran. Right after that, she died. I quit my job that day and took the train to Chicago."

Coop has been hiding from real moments his entire life. That's how he was trained. His mom thought it was best if he pretended not to have this gift, one that people would abuse. His alcoholic dad thought he had great instinct and hoped his son didn't have this curse. His father would marvel at his ability to hit a baseball but questioned how he couldn't make a free throw. His father deemed him lazy and worthless; his mother knew the truth and helped him create a system to stay out of trouble.

With a quick glance, Natalie knows he's thinking about his mom. "I'm sorry about your mother. I don't need to be rescued; I need company."

"It's my nature not to trust, especially someone with legs that could wrap around a man twice, and those eyes."

Trying to get Coop comfortable, "And you like my boobs. I'm staying a few blocks away with a friend from college. You want to see me, call me. I'm not trying to recruit you. I don't want to be saved. I'm leaving the country in a few weeks. It would be nice to see you before I leave."

Concern replaces the feeling of mistrust. Coop can see it, but Natalie never makes it to Australia. Coop shares zero details. He tries to focus on her warmth and beauty. She's okay with his gawking. "I do like your boobs."

A serious look returns on Natalie's face, "I sense emotion. I know how and why people are feeling happy, sad, or distrusting. I'm not the strongest five percent, but I stayed out of trouble for years. I can't pick stocks, and I don't always know how the market is going to swing but it's true what they say, emotional market. My boss knew I had some sort of gift, but she thought it was my research. She used me to get rich."

Feeling safe, Coop opens up, "I know what people want to hear. I'm not always perfect but numbers, cards, patterns, pop into my brain quickly. I couldn't pick all six lotto numbers, but I could get four. That's why baseball worked for me. I knew the pitch."

Impressed and surprised, Natalie stares at binders Coop brought with him, "Who does all this research?"

"I have someone. The handwriting and labeling always give it away. I have not had a single person look at this crap and guess the handwriting was mine. My researcher, Nina, needs the money and it looks real. She is also learning a ton. I see a glimpse of her future, and she does some amazing things."

Natalie hasn't felt this comfortable in years. "I've never spoken to anyone about this. It feels good. I had no idea until college that I had this gift. My parents just thought I was smart with a high emotional IQ. I aced all my exams; only thing I did was go to class. I studied but only the material I noticed the teacher passionately discussing."

Coop responds with a smile, "I totally get it. I'm so lucky that I did not have to spend hours studying. My mom figured it out when I was five. She had these math cards. I remember it was addition. We never did math before, but I knew all the answers. She smiled and told me that I was smart. And then she started crafting a plan."

While Natalie chats about growing up in Boston, Coop remembers how sly his mom was. She made him focus on learning, not on "cheating" with his mind. She encouraged failure and lectured him daily on how to control his skills, "One day this amazing gift might fade, so it's important you learn and fail. You will have to work extremely hard to control reading thoughts. Bad people will take advantage of you." His life was planned out to avoid others knowing he was in the 5%. He made sure to get an occasional B on a test, kept his batting percentage under .400, couldn't play games on his phone, and had to learn martial arts.

Sensing Coop's distance, Natalie asks, "What are you thinking about?"

Without going into detail, "My mom. At age five, she put me in baseball, martial arts and basketball. I loved fighting, hated baseball, and sucked at basketball."

11

"Why didn't you quit baseball?"

"It was a way to pay for college. My mom was afraid if my test scores were too high the government would snatch me away. And baseball came easy. I generally knew which pitch to swing at. I set a college record my junior year for getting the most walks. My mom was pissed. She thought I was using my skill unfairly. The truth was, even though I knew what pitch was coming, I still couldn't hit it. Those pitchers can whip it."

Laughing and comforting Coop, "I get it—blending in is not always easy. I remember knowing that my best friend from college got knocked up the day she had sex. That was really when I knew I had a gift. I convinced her to take the day-after pill. She hated me, but she smoked a lot of weed, loved drinking and was only eighteen."

Coop adds with a smile, "I wish I had the ability to know when a girl could not get pregnant."

"You are nasty. That's my cue. This was really nice." Meeting Coop halfway, Natalie gives him a short, but sweet, kiss. Coop wishes he could think happy thoughts, because that was a great kiss, but concern takes over. If the CIA wanted to find her, they would've. Someone else is tracking her. And she honestly doesn't know it.

"Be safe, Natalie. You know how to fight?"

Looking puzzled, "What?" After repeating his question, "I took a little cardio kickboxing."

With a concerned tone, "Tomorrow we train. Basic stuff to help you out in a jam."

Natalie smiles at Coop as she walks out. Starring into space, Coop sees his mom, Emma Cooper. She worried this would happen. He can hear her warm voice warning him, "Don't be a hero. Be a gentleman; take care of people but don't be a hero." She would make a joke out of it, "Comic book heroes are dangerously depressed and live a lonely life. Just look at Bruce Wayne."

Picking up his cell, "Sammy, aren't you still on a date?"

"She just left. Man, I owe you. Shelly is amazing. Like no woman I've met in my life. She has no filter, no fear, no games.

And the sex. It's like porn. I had no idea that flexibility like that existed. She can stand up and lift her leg on top of my shoulder. I owe you."

"Cool. Why don't you buy some steaks for dinner? I'll grill when I finish working. And we can watch some of the tourney."

"Perfect." Putting down his cell and concentrating on his work, Coop tries to drown out thoughts of Natalie.

RUNNING AWAY

Natalie throws another load of laundry in her friend Karen's machine. Karen sits on the couch recovering from a rough night of drinking. Her usual hangover cure is reality television, Advil, grilled cheese, and a Gatorade.

Natalie remarks, "You look like you're recovering from biking a hundred miles."

With a naturally deep voice, "This system has worked for years. So, I have no stomach lining, but I'm still able to tolerate cheese. And I'll take that as a win. How was Mr. Handsome?"

"He is amazing. I think I want to marry him. But he just wants to sleep with me."

Karen turns down the volume on the television because reality is better than reality television. "Did you sleep with him? You are such a little slut. Sunday afternoon sex. That's what you do with your husband before you have kids. Not some stranger."

Shocked by her friend's comment, "I'm not a slut! We kissed. It was this short, sweet kiss. His dreamy lips melted me. I almost fell! My damn right knee went out and I had to walk really slow, so I didn't fall on my ass."

Questions continue to be shot at Natalie. "What's next? When are you going to see Mr. Handsome again?"

"Tomorrow! What do you wear to a boxing lesson?" Discussing wardrobe options as she folds laundry, Natalie contemplates postponing her trip to Australia. She leaves in two weeks, but what's one more week? She could probably stay at Coop's—or would that be too presumptuous?

Coop uses classical music and stock analysis to avoid thoughts of Natalie. The occasional thought crosses his mind, like a commercial break. Could he go to Australia with her? Things were much easier for him when he waited at the bar for a girl that he knew only wanted sex. It always surprised him just how many women want sex and maybe cuddling.

Pulling up his laptop, Coop realizes this is his week to make a bad trade. His organizational skills are unmatched. Emma was an excellent mom and an even better professional organizer. Whether you wanted a closet or filing cabinet, Emma was your woman. And she made sure Coop had a system. His intricate plan for school varied week to week and class to class. When he would get an occasional B, it had to seem random, even though it was planned from the start of the semester. Baseball, judo, fencing, and even board games had to show "performance variance." For almost 30 years, this strategy kept him flying under the radar. Natalie could not ruin his life plan.

Running away is Natalie's current life plan. As she packs her bags and maps out her trip, the only certainty in her mind is that she can never come back.

CASH MONEY

Basketball and steaks are a perfect combination for Sunday night. March Madness is Sam's favorite time of the year. His office has a pool, his friends have a pool, and he always does the CBS contest. This year, with a little guilt and Coop's picks, he's doing really well.

The tournament is something Coop does not fully see. He can guess the final three teams easily, and half the time he can pick the winner. That's not a hypothetical number; Coop tracks it. He has the version for his friends, and then he has another version he keeps just for curiosity. Even though he doesn't want anyone to know his secret, he likes to test out how accurate his mind works. The version for his friends is always a top four finisher, but if he won every year, someone would ask questions.

Coop lets the steaks rest before serving. Although he's no master chef, Coop has some kitchen skills. He started cooking at noon. His mom would usually see clients right after he came home from school. Emma would leave out the ingredients and tell Coop what to do. Usually, dinner came out well. Her famous line was, "If it sucks, we order pizza." Sometimes Coop hoped it would suck so he could get pizza.

"Sammy, grab me two beers, I'll take your iPad to the couch." Coop immediately senses Sammy's fear. Sammy is afraid Coop will look at the screen and notice that all the winners in the tournament are Coop's. "What's up, Sammy? Why do you look so stressed?"

With an apologetic look, "I stole your picks in the tourney. Every single game, if we win, I promise to give you all or maybe half. I told Shelly that I would give you whatever you wanted."

Trying to control his anger, Coop bangs his hand on his grey, granite island. "Fuck. Don't answer the phone."

Sammy's cell phone buzzes five seconds later, "Why? How did you know that was going to happen?"

"It vibrated on the table before it rang. I'm not that good, but I knew they would call you."

Sammy's look of confusion pushes Coop to fess up. "You want to know why I did so well in college without studying, why I knew that Shelly would go home with you, why I know three out of the four Final Four teams every year? I'm in the five percent. And now your life is in danger."

Sammy's long fingers cover his pale face, as he nervously runs his hands through his buzz cut. "Fuck. I knew it. I knew there was some reason you never lost more than a few hundred in Vegas. All these years, the few times you lost a bet, and you just never get upset. Because you knew you were going to lose. How did I not figure this out? I just thought you were the greatest wingman on the face of the planet. Why am I in trouble?"

"The guys who organize these contests are looking for the five percent. It's usually the mob. They take the winners and exploit their talent. That voicemail is someone calling about the contest. A guy, trying to figure out if you are in the five percent."

Sammy, still in shock, "How am I so stupid? We've lived next to each other for two years. We hung out all the time in college. "

Coop tries to relax and think of the next steps; he knew that something like this could happen. Sammy replays major events in his head. "Now Vegas for Kenny's wedding makes total sense. You made us play roulette at four different casinos. You won us all a few grand. We called it the luckiest night ever. How did no one figure it out?"

"Calm down. I've had decades of practice fooling people. It has not been easy hiding this, but it was for your protection. Please take a bite of this steak and let me think."

The filet is cooked perfectly. The juice runs down the plate with each cut. Sammy's mind cannot focus, "I was going to give you the money so you could open up a restaurant. You've talked about a taco stand in Hawaii since we met. Or a bar. I was going to help you make it happen."

Coop's mind starts working. The contest screeners will call and ask Sammy some questions. They will realize it was random luck. To be safe, he'll run some interference on the call just in case they try to read Sammy's mind. Shit, if it doesn't work, they move. "Relax, Sammy. I've been preparing for this my whole life."

Sammy, confused and embarrassed, "Tell me what's next?"

"Just let me know if you get any emails or calls about the contest. And if you do, you tell them it was all luck. You won't be lying. You're lucky you saw my picks. I'm going to keep a look out and we'll be fine." Sammy starts eating his steak and calms down. Coop starts to make a mental list of what he needs to do.

"I'm so sorry, Coop."

PREPPING

Motion detector lights are not new for the walk up to Coop's place, but the cameras are new. They are wireless, and all the movements are tracked and stored in the cloud. Coop will get an update on his phone every time they are triggered. Baseball bats, which Coop had anyway, are stowed beneath his bed and Sammy's. Maybe this is all for nothing, but protecting Sammy is goal number one. This wonderful friend and neighbor has been like a brother to Coop. And when his mom died, the only real friend he had was Sammy. He knew one day he would have to tell Sammy. Shockingly, he feels relieved. He's known Sammy almost six years, and he's practically family.

Coop suddenly feels responsible for Nina and Natalie, too. His mom warned him that one day he might need to use his gift to protect those he cares about. That's one of the reasons they practiced strengthening his mind. Coop will never forget his after homework, special training. Emma would drill him with questions. With a stern but sweet voice, "Jay, what did Bobby wear to school today? What was he nervous about? You must be a great observer of life, son. What number am I thinking of right now? What color? How many fingers am I holding behind my back?" The rapid-fire questions made Coop feel like he was on a game show. He would get prizes for correct answers. The drills were fun for him. Getting bad grades on purpose was more of a challenge. He always overthought which question to bomb, and then time ran out and that was that. He loved multiple choice tests the best. His system was easy: After completing the test, he would go back and randomly change three or more answers.

As Coop cleans up the mess from drilling holes for cameras, he goes back to his mom's superhero routine, "Don't be a hero. Seriously, look at Batman; he lives a horrible life of depression and isolation. And that poor Peter Parker; he never got the girl or accolades. I know you think I'm being funny, but avengers die every day." Coop can't help smiling.

Natalie is doing her own prep for travel. Reading up on Australia has been her hobby for the past two weeks. She's read every travel guide in the library and spent hours surfing the web for travel information. Her temporary roommate, Karen, spent a semester in Sydney and is going on and on about the zoo.

"I get it. I will visit the zoo. Hey, I'm going to meet my new friend for a self-defense lesson; you never told me what to wear!"

Being a fashion-conscious girl, Karen digs through her closet and offers, "keep it simple, Lululemon pants will make your butt look great, black sports bra and pink tee over it. You still have to be girly."

"Have I told you how much I love you? You should come with me!"

Shaking her head no, "This is your date. Right? Is this a date? Are you in the friend zone?"

With a smile, "Coop might end up just being a friend, but I think he wants a little more than that. You don't kiss your friends."

CLASS STARTS

Nina lets herself in like usual. She takes off her shoes, wheels in her suitcase/filing cabinet and lets out a yell, "Coop. I'm here!" Her next step: grabbing a giant cup of coffee and a banana. Usually, Coop and Sammy are eating breakfast.

Sammy never came to breakfast. Extreme guilt and worry forced him to make his own breakfast. However, Coop went to him. With a sandwich and a smile, "Sammy, act natural. It's not the end of the world."

"I think I'm more shocked that you came to me. This is like the third time in two years you've stopped by."

With a quick retort, "Clean up and maybe cook something for me. Actually, you once baked cookies. Those were awesome." Coop is trying to calm Sammy down. He knew he would be uneasy the next few days, and any reassurance will help.

Running downstairs, Coop sees his door is slightly ajar. He closed and locked the door not even five minutes ago. His heart races as he steps in, then he quickly lets out a sigh. "Fuck, you scared the crap out of me. I saw your mini loafers and immediately relaxed."

Shaking her head, "I'm short. Did you expect big loafers? Let's get down to business. I have to meet a professor this morning."

Trying not to pry or read her mind, Coop says, "Okay, boss. What do you have for me?" Nina opens her file cabinet on wheels and pulls out a few files. Her record keeping and organizational skills are unparalleled. Everyone says in the interview, "I'm organized," but he knew Nina meant it. She tracks all his trades and compares him to 20 other traders and a dozen market indicators, like the S&P 500. Since that was extremely easy for her to do, Coop now has her research various companies.

With her usual serious tone, "You are doing well this quarter. Up twenty-four percent. Pretty awesome. Last year at this time you were at a subpar six percent, which did not beat the market. The greatest losers are in red and the next in green. I recommend dumping the ones in red and holding the green. You have a good amount of liquid assets sitting around. Might want to invest while the market is hot." Before Coop can ask for suggestions, Nina carries on, "I compiled a list of companies with the biggest upswing. Using your forecasting model, the ones in blue are winners; the yellow tabs are companies I recommend further research."

Coop's mother always wanted him to have proof. With her warm smile she would review homework and ask, "Where is the proof? How did you come to this conclusion? People are going to ask you, Jay, how you came to this number. Life requires evidence, proof, for everything you do." With Emma's voice in his head, he spent months studying financial forecasting, reading journals, papers, and lots of YouTube. Although Nina is getting her master's in finance, Coop taught her his system and it's very sophisticated.

"Thanks for your recommendations. How is school?"

"That's why you pay me. It's going well. I forwarded you a few emails with links to interesting articles. You know, if you get more capital, we could probably make millions in about three years. These private equity firms don't want you unless you can invest at least ten million."

"Nina, there is no doubt you will manage millions of dollars. That is not my goal. I want enough cash to bank roll a restaurant, or maybe just a few food trucks."

Nina thinks everyone wants to be a multi-millionaire. "What is a matter with you, Coop? You have all this talent. Your instincts, combined with my research, man, we could be ballers."

"Listen, little baller, I just want to be happy. Money only takes you so far."

With a divas smile, "Yea, like all around the world. I want to be space travel rich. I have no idea why. Is that wrong? I don't care about nice cars, fancy clothes, or a huge house. I just want to have hundreds of millions of dollars in the bank. And P.S., my rapper name was little baller."

"Go back to school. I'll cut a check Friday. You millennials crack me up."

While Nina walks to the door, she notices a green raincoat on the coat rack. "Jay Cooper has a lady friend. Nice color. Is she hiding?"

Coop enjoys his privacy, "Bye, Nina. I'll tell the owner of the coat you approve."

Looking down at his watch, Coop realizes that Natalie will be here in thirty minutes. He runs down to the basement, searching for his old pads and punching bag. Talking to himself, "is this too much?" Grabbing a pair of Thai boxing pads, and leaving the other crap on the floor, he heads back to his place, the entire time reassuring himself, "This is just a friendly thing to do. No sex, no emotions. Just help this girl kick her way out of trouble."

All he can see is her butt and the back of her long brown hair. "Hi, Natalie. I'm right behind you."

With a hug, Natalie asks, "What are those red pads?"

"They are for you to kick and hit. I wrap them around my forearms, and, hopefully, they absorb your badass moves. Aside from your fists, anything can be a weapon: keys, a book—you can smash it into the temples."

With a smile, Natalie responds, "Good times!"

Natalie places a caring hand on Coop's face, "This is really sweet of you." Resisting the urge to kiss, they both nervously smile instead. It has been a long time since Natalie has been attracted to someone. Her last relationship ended two years ago, and he was a sweet boy, and that was the problem. He never matured. Coop, on the other hand, has never had a long relationship. Sure, there have been girls he's dated for a few months, but his wall never comes down. Eventually the women get sick of knowing nothing about him.

With a serious look, "I'm going to teach you how to elbow, knee and smack someone. I'll also show an escape from a bear hug and choke." Picking up on her nervousness, "I will be playing the bear. You might like it."

With a big flirty smile, "I will like it. Where did you learn this stuff? You teach others? Can you show me how to shoot a gun?"

Nodding his head yes, "My mom made me take a bunch of martial arts. My dad taught me how to fire guns and rifles when I was little. It was freaky. Since he had a drinking problem—which he called silencing the voices in his head—it was a little scary. With his hands shaking, he'd hand me a gun, tell me how to load it, turn the safety off, hold my breath as I aim, and fire. Given my young age and the fear that his breath could start a fire, I learned that lesson quickly. My only other trainee is Sam, my best friend. What about your parents?"

As Natalie describes her working-class parents, Coop demonstrates the first way to throw an elbow. Without interrupting, he points to where the elbow should land, pointing to his nose, his chin butt, cheek bones, temples, and sternum.

Natalie jams the elbow against the pads with ease. While moving her elbow up, down, across, and back, she asks a serious question, "So what happened with your dad?"

"He was a mess. He worked in security for the city. He was a cop but couldn't stand the dirty cops; which is funny, because he didn't seem too honest. When I was about six, he vanished. I still remember the cold winter night. He came into my room; it was late. His breath smelled like vodka mixed with coffee; it was nasty. He kissed my forehead, which was his thing, and said, 'You're better off without me.' And even at that age, I knew it was true. I had no idea that meant he was never coming back."

Coop takes a deep breath and changes the subject, "Who's after you? It's not the government."

Coop reads her mind as she honestly answers, "I have no idea. They said they were CIA. They said my boss, Mary Stern, was up to no good. We worked for Benz and Cohen Investing. My job was to research global companies; Matthew Benz worked domestically, and Art Cohen advised nonprofits on investing strategies."

Coop's mind starts buzzing. International spies, global governments with organized crime, weak economies with a strong leader, poor country with militant leader.

Sammy knocks on the door and then comes running in, slightly out of breath. Watching a woman driving her knee into a pad over Coop's face does not faze Sammy. "I got a message. Listen to it."

"Hi, Mr. Linch. Congrats on your excellent bracket. My name is Fred. I work with CBS and want to talk to you about the next few weeks of the tournament. If you win, there will be photo shoots; I need to check dates and some other details. I know this seems premature, but we like to have a system because everything happens quickly after the final game ends. Call me at this number ..."

Coop seems a little relieved, "Ok. I'm going to call Fred. You can go back to work. I think this will work out. And this is Natalie."

Sam goes for a handshake, but Natalie forces a hug. Sam's heart rate starts to drop. After all the freaking out earlier this week, Sam might be able to sleep tonight. The array of different emotions Natalie sensed when Sam walked in is crazy. He's suddenly calm, relaxed, and sincere. And he compliments Natalie while walking out, "Great to meet you. Nice elbow. You might be the nicest guest Coop has ever introduced me to. Are you a model?"

Smiling, "Thank you, Sam! I'll take those compliments."

As Sammy leaves, Coop removes his gloves and jots down notes. Natalie takes a sip of water and offers to leave. Coop fights the urge to ravage her; that's his only thought as he stares at her dimples, and then her breasts. "Before you leave, one question—are those real?"

"Since we've known each other for a little over seventy-two hours, I'll tell you the truth." Pausing for effect, "Yes, they are real. You can touch them. Maybe after you buy me dinner." Continuing to flirt with her body signals, she pulls Coop towards her with a finger. Trying to resist with all his strength, he caves.

A perfect kiss ruins him. He's not supposed to fall in love. He's not supposed to be a hero. Letting Natalie leave his apartment is not easy. She wanted to stay, and he knew it. On a positive note, he sees her future change. She does get to Australia, or at least the airport. That's a start.

RESEARCH

Usually, Coop would pass this kind of work on to Nina, but investigating Benz and Cohen could get dicey. Why, why is someone tracking Natalie, and what does she know? She is living with an old college friend. It's only a matter of time before they find her. The question is, who are "they?"

Coop heads out to a nearby computer shop. He purchases a used laptop and heads to the West Loop. Sitting down at a coffee shop, Coop begins researching Benz, who also does international investments. Their website includes strategy and countries they invest in. Before leaving Starbucks, Coop places a small wireless camera on the wall. He's confident whoever the mystery men are, they will find him, but maybe he can get a visual before they knock on his door.

Although Coop calmed Sammy down, he's still scared. He grew up in Lincoln, Nebraska; the biggest concern there was the Cornhuskers season. Feeling very comfortable with his new girlfriend, Sam packs a bag and heads over for a few nights. He explains, "I messed up. Coop is a little annoyed with me. Can I stay with you for a night?"

With no hesitation, "Of course! This means marriage soon, because I live with my sister, and she will tell my parents. My parents will mysteriously show up on Friday and apply pressure." Half laughing, half serious, "As long as you leave by Friday morning, you'll be okay."

Usually talk of marriage, even jest, scares the crap out of Sammy. He has not committed to any female relationship for longer than six months. Of course, that tops Coop's endless array of one-night stands.

After a slightly awkward pause, Sam says, "I'm okay with that."

OLD MAN

Coop seldom drives. He has an older Pontiac GTO. After cooking, cars are his second love. He found this one online a few years ago and decided it would be nice to occasionally drive something other than a rental car.

Sammy uses the car more than he does. Sammy reminds his friend, "The trunk is perfect for Costco or dead bodies." With Sam shacking-up with Shelly and Natalie packing, Coop drives out to the Southside for more research.

Benz and Cohen Investing have so many transactions, that, even using his gift, Coop is having trouble narrowing down what country would be after Natalie. Traveling with her boss, Mary, Natalie visited Europe with the most frequency. It's probably a country in that continent or nearby. Benz and Cohen Investing made $600 million investing in companies around the Ukraine. And her company thanked Natalie Barns for her excellent instincts in the international market.

Leaving another camera in this coffee shop, Coop heads home. Spending all this time viewing tape is putting him to sleep. Taking a few gulps of coffee gives him the jolt he needs to drive home.

As Coop pulls his car in the driveway, he notices a man in a blazer, khakis, and a bowler hat pacing near his condo. Combined with the aviator sunglasses, the man looks out of the '70s. Noticing no one else around, Coop yells in the stranger's direction. "Hey, can I help you?"

An unusual feeling overcomes Coop; he knows this guy. The stranger comments, "I'm looking for Sam Linch."

Immediately Coop knows this person is looking for him. "You must be Jay Cooper."

A tear forms in Coop's eye—not out of fear, but raw emotion. "How did you find me, Dad? Should I call you Fred or Ted?"

Pointing to his house, "Let's go inside and chat. Dad, Fred, whatever you want." Coop has practiced this meeting before. He knew exactly what he wanted to say to this no-good asshole that left him before he turned seven and never returned. This alcoholic scum bag is now working for the mob. How fitting.

"Jay, relax your mind."

"Are you fucking kidding me? Relax? It's been about twenty years." Taking a deep breath and trying to control his emotions, "You are in the five percent?" While his father takes off his hat and glasses, he looks almost identical to the way Jay remembered him. Squinty eyes, almost bald, salt and pepper beard, and still smirking, he's aged slightly better than expected.

"Listen kid, I had to leave. They were starting to figure out the five percent, and if it was hereditary. I knew you had the gift but hoped I was wrong. You had that analytical look in your eye, even as a baby. Trying to figure out what was going to happen next."

"Well, what the fuck am I thinking about now?"

"Some girl, and me. Let me tell you, it was not easy leaving. I wanted you to be a baseball player. Shit, in college you led the NCAA in walks, what the fuck? You could've been a great hitter. I just wanted that for you. Had you stayed that course, none of this shit would be happening." Coop stares at his dad in disbelief, how did he know about his college baseball career?

"Don't look so shocked. I know everything about you. Your mom raised you to be James Bond. Four languages, more martial arts than Bruce Lee, but she always stressed not to be a hero. It was odd. She prepared you for this the best she could. She had no idea how hard it is to block out the voices. To pretend you don't know the right answer. Man, she planned everything for you. Developed this system to fake everyone out, but then she made you work on your craft."

Coop's curiosity is piqued, "Practice? She just helped me with a schedule to succeed, while you drank and showed your six-year-old son how to fire a gun."

Coop remembers firing round after round into an old tire. His dad made him load the gun, turn off the safety and fire until the chamber emptied, then move on to the next piece of equipment. "Oh, and you even had me throw knives, so maybe you were training me for this role."

"Dead wrong. I knew that all the kung-fu in the world couldn't stop a bullet. Emma would have you practice reading the minds of people in restaurants, in the street. Don't you remember hobo homework? You had to tell her if the homeless man was on drugs, crazy, or legitimately needed money for food. And yeah, I drank. You get it. You hear all that shit in your head. Everyone's bullshit. Now I have to cover up for your roommate's screw-up. How the hell did he get your tourney picks?"

"I had them on my computer. No idea he was snooping. Not usually in his DNA. I don't need your help. GO! Tell your mob buddies I'm the culprit."

"Don't be stupid. This case is over. I'll tell them Sammy got lucky. End of story. There's a million other losers I need to track down. Unless he wins."

The hurt and anger filling up Coop's body is obvious, even if you're not in the 5%. "Jay, I wanted to protect you. Your mom and I never married to keep you safe. My name is not on your birth certificate to protect you. Believe it or not, I left to protect you. They are hunting down the five percent in Albania. They run tests on us. Horrible Nazi shit. Draining blood, and placing it in another's body. Stem cell research. In the U.S., they are too busy using us to make money. Chances are that's who's coming for your girlfriend. Better tell her to leave now."

Coop's blood pressure and breath begin to settle. "How strong is your gift?"

"Nothing like yours. I have visions. It's like a short movie. I sense emotion but I can't tell you what you're going to say or pick the lottery numbers. I remember you were amazing. You could guess five out of six lotto numbers right before the drawing. It was ridiculous. However, the day before, you could maybe get four consistently. Your greatest gift was instinct. That's why you were so good at baseball, boxing, and foreign language. When your mind started working, you could figure anything out. It was amazing how fast you learned math. Once you got the basics you kept digging. You couldn't turn off emotion; that's what I can do. That's why I was able to leave the greatest thing I ever did. And I knew you would never forgive me. That's what sucked the most. I know you think I'm horrible, a loser, an alcoholic, all true. But I will die protecting you." Tears run down Fred's face.

Trying to hold back his emotions, "Dad, helping me is not going to erase the years of pain. Wondering what happened, where you were. I had no idea if you drank yourself to death. I thought it was my fault you left, and it kind of is. If mom never got pregnant you would've had a great life. I never asked to be born. I played by her rules and now it's time to see if she really prepared me for this."

The old man puts his head down in shame, "There's one thing. If Sam wins this pool. Someone will be back. You should plan an exit strategy."

Trying to contain the hate, Jack sees Fred's going to get shot. The image confuses him. Fred sees a similar vision, but it's his son bleeding. He's not going to let that happen.

Pointing to the door, Fred gets the message. Before walking out of the driveway, Fred picks up his phone, "Yea it's me. Sam Linch is one lucky son of a bitch. Who's next?"

ALBANIA

Trying to relax, Coop walks around the city. His only interruption is a pleasant one, "Hi, Coop. Did I leave two rings in your house?"

Natalie's warm voice acts like a sedative. Coop asks, "I don't think so. Can I stop by?"

Even through the phone Natalie reads Coop's emotions, "Of course. Come by sixteen twenty-four North Lincoln Avenue."

"Listen—don't freak out, but I'm outside your place. I've been walking around town for an hour. I guess my mind knew you were here, and I need you." Fighting back crocodile tears, Coop leans against the door. Anger bubbles up inside of him. A tight hug from Natalie and all the emotion comes out. "All this time, I thought he was dead. I thought he had to be dead to walk out on us. He says it was for protection. He was trying to keep us safe. Despite the crazy gun lessons, the vodka breath, the short-fused temper, he was still my father. I survived without him. Fuck him."

Walking inside Natalie's friend's house, Coop tries to choke back the tears. "Don't worry, Coop. Karen is out for the night."

Blocking out his drama, "Thank you for that. For listening." Trying to compose himself, "You have to leave tonight. Someone figured out you have a gift. It was a company overseas. Your track record was impeccable. Too good. They thought your boss was the gifted one. According to my dad, it's Albanians. They will find you. See you went to Drake. Find out you were a Kappa, and that Karen was your roommate."

With a surprising smile, "I want one more day with you."

Lifting Natalie up on top of a dresser, Coop reaches in for a kiss. She unbuttons his shirt and puts her hand on his scarred shoulders, and immediately feels his pain. Without her saying a word, "Baseball is hard on the shoulders."

Coop smiles, "I'm fine."

Slowly lifting her shirt, Coop's initial assessment was correct, "They are perfect." They both laugh as Coop cups her breasts and smiles as he nuzzles them. His light beard tickles. Wrapping her long legs around Coop, he carries her over to the bed.

Fred Smith is at a bar settling in for the night. Instead of vodka on ice, he orders a soda water with a lime. Twenty-plus years since he last spoke to his son was a mistake. A choice he made that his wife disagreed with. Maybe she was right. A boy needs a father, but not an abusive alcoholic that sees the future one frame at a time. He didn't know how to father, and visions of Jay getting hurt were deeply imbedded in his mind. Fred couldn't separate normal parent concern, like falling off a bike, from the crazy visions that constantly buzzed in his head. Although not there as a parent, his gambling cash was delivered to the house every month. Maybe if he didn't win so much, he wouldn't be working for the mob and government.

GREAT SEX

Figuring out how to please his lovers was Coop's goal. Most of the time, he was able to gauge positions, tempo, and force. It was a sport, and he had no trouble using his edge to impress the opposite sex. Dirty talk had somehow become his specialty. Whispering dirty or sweet nothings seemed to really help his dates enjoy the tryst.

With Natalie, it was effortless. She knows how he likes his back scratched with her long nails. She can feel his endorphins rise as she firmly kisses his neck and tightly squeezes his bubble butt. "You are killing me, girl." With all these amazing sensations, Coop feels like a rookie. The only pleasure he can sense is how she likes her back to be lightly tickled and her neck and ears kissed. Without completely losing himself, Coop resorts to breathing techniques. With every thrust, Coop takes a deep breath in, holds for a four count and exhales.

Feeling neglected, "Jay, fuck me. I don't care if you cum."

And just like that, Coop flips Natalie on her back and drives into her fast while lightly biting her bottom lip. With a big smile and moan, Natalie whispers, "That's it. Come on. Oh my GOD! You are good at this!"

With a huge grin and a little out of breath, "Thanks. You're pretty amazing."

Sammy is having similar luck with Shelly. Earlier in the night he received a text from Coop and it eased his concern about the tournament. After reading that text, it's as if a giant weight was temporarily removed from his back and he could breathe easy again.

Shelly's apartment is cute. Since her sister travels often for work, she lives mostly alone. The high-rise building feels safe, and it's not far from the loop. Although her unit is small, it has two bedrooms, great windows and she can easily walk to work. Sammy brought clothes for work, hoping to sleep over for a few nights.

Another round of sex in the morning makes it difficult for Coop to tell Natalie that she needs to leave immediately. "I have never met anyone that cares like you. Not just the sex, but you have an amazing heart. I want to meet you at the top of the Great Barrier Reef. It should take you about three weeks if you stop along the way, take trains and busses, and enjoy the country. You should leave now."

"Jay Cooper, aka, Coop, you find me in the Outback." After dressing for the day, Natalie pulls out a huge suitcase already packed. "I'm one step ahead of you. My ride will be here soon. I like you, Coop. I'm going to be,"

Coop interrupts with a hand, "Don't tell me. In case I run into another crazy person that reads minds, I don't want them to find this."

With a smile, "I'm traveling like a tourist. You'll find me."

Picking Natalie up and squeezing her like a protective lover, "Elbow, knee, kick to the knee. I'll see you down under, if you know what I mean."

THE FINAL FOUR

The spring night is unusually cold. Puffy coats and scarves litter tables in the bars. All eyes are glued to the Michigan game. Unlike most people, Sammy and Coop hope their bracket busts. Coop selected Syracuse to win the game, not because he's a fan, but that's what popped in his head. If they win, Sammy will be tied for first place heading into the final four.

Nina, who could care less about basketball, is studying at Coop's house. Her girlfriend, Tonya, is throwing a party at their apartment, Nina wanted a quiet place to study. Most employees would not hang out at their boss's house, but Nina is like a little sister to Coop. Her salary for an analyst is ridiculously high, and she also shares in the profits. Coop has been grooming her to take over the business. With all uncertainty hanging over him like a rain cloud, Coop might need to speed up the transition plan.

Nina's mind works like a scientific calculator. All the formulas teachers allow students to bring with them for exams, Nina memorizes. She is not in the 5%, but her intelligence is off the charts. Coop spotted her waiting tables. Her eyes were glued to the stock ticker as she delivered Coop's turkey club. She will never forget Coop's response to how's your sandwich, "Tell me what IBM is doing right now; I'll hire you and pay you fifty thousand plus a bonus." The very next day she started, and within a few months she picked up Coop's trading philosophy.

Yelling, not because he's angry but because the bar is so loud, "Sam, where's your girl?"

"Not sure. She is not a fan of day drinking. She's probably at home watching the game."

While texting Shelly, whose status is already girlfriend, Coop wonders how Natalie is. He hopes she has made it out of Chicago, lying on a warm beach. And hopefully she does not know the results from her boss's autopsy. The crazy workaholic overdosed on an unlisted medication, which means someone killed her.

Fred is also watching the game, praying Sam does not win. Although he works for the government, he's done some shady things for Sports Game Inc. They use brutality, spying, cheating, and rarely lose money. They run contests, take out insurance money to cover any loss, and locate the 5% while doing so. Once they find out someone is in the 5%, they are immediately wined and dined. And the money is tempting but if you cross them, you end up on the back of a milk carton. Fred walks a fine line, but he's so gifted, they don't pay attention to all the extracurricular activities he does.

Coop watches the game closely. Despite Syracuse being down by 14 with three minutes left, he knows they will win. His other final four teams are Michigan State, Indiana, and Duke.

The bartender, Sal, leans in and asks Coop, "I'll give you Indiana by two."

"Sal, you know I hate taking your money. We've been through this all winter. I'm in. The usual?"

The usual bet is one hundred dollars, and these two friends bet on everything. Sal doesn't have a gambling problem, just a boredom issue. He made millions at a tech firm and then bought the bar. According to Coop, Sal lives the dream.

"Alright, Coop. What if we up the ante? Two fifty? I got a solid tip, and I know you like the Hoosiers."

While they argue over the bet, Shelly walks in. She somehow looks more beautiful each time Sam sees her. Her orange Syracuse sweatshirt makes her blue eyes pop, and her black leggings perfect-ly highlight her defined legs. Most importantly, Sammy has never been happier.

Coop comments, "Shelly, I thought you were an East Coast girl. The accent is pretty slight. Sammy, would you move out there?"

Sammy answers with no hesitation, "Why not. You'd visit, right?" Coop offers a huge smile while nodding yes.

As Syracuse beats Michigan, the entire bar, minus the handful of alums, explodes with excitement. Coop hides his disappoint-ment, trying to convince himself he has three shots left of being wrong.

With a fake smile, Coop turns to Sammy and Shelly, "Smoked brisket? I have a ton on the smoker, and Nina always drops off cookies when she stops by."

With one look at Shelly, Coop knows that Sammy told her everything. He figured that would happen. Selling Sammy on moving out will be easier with Shelly in the picture. She'll take care of him while he finds a place.

Shelly accepts before Sammy can reply, "Count me in! How did you learn how to cook? First the omelet, now barbeque? You're going to spoil a girl."

Rubbing his brown locks, "My mom taught me how to cook. Not the conventional way. Back before there were a bunch of food channels, PBS had cooking shows. My mom's attempt to strength-en my mind involved cooking shows and the science guy. I think I was around nine when my mom first made me watch these shows and tell her what the next ingredient was before the chef said it. I had to also tell her the amount."

Sammy butts in, "When you told me your mom taught you to cook, I pictured a recipe, you on a step stool, and your mom handing you flour."

Coop continues with a smile, "That's only the half of it. The show we watched was on Sundays. She wrote down the recipe and then kept it hidden. The following week I had to make the dish with no recipe. It really helped develop my memory, cooking skills, and how I organize thoughts."

Shelly, very inquisitive, "What happened if you screwed up?"

"Good question. One time I used coconut oil instead of coconut milk. The smell was great, but it tasted as if I was trying to poison us. My mom didn't get upset but she sternly told me, life is about the details."

Interrupting Jay's warm fuzzy memory, Shelly's line of questioning continues, "Did you know I would like Sammy? Did you see us together? How often have you gotten Sam laid?"

Having known Shelly all of 10 days, her directness does not shock Sammy. He likes it; he's always needed a woman that could help him make quicker decisions, keep him motivated, and ask the questions he's afraid to ask.

While slicing the brisket and trying to avoid cutting off a finger, "The moment I saw you, I knew Sammy would fall in love with you a little too quick, but you would do the same. You wanted a sweet man, genuine, and you are a sucker for blonds with nice butts. Sammy is also a sucker for that look. I have often tried and failed at getting Sammy laid. With sports, he's assertive; with women, not so much. But I knew you were on a mission. You wanted to meet someone that night, but I have no idea why. Spill the beans."

Curious and quiet, Sammy and Coop await Shelly's response. "The truth is, I bumped into my ex. He had this gorgeous Latin girl practically in his lap." With her stern look morphing into a smile, "I wanted the same thing, but a Norwegian instead."

Sammy responds, "I'll take that as a compliment."

Back with her line of questions, "Has your memory ever failed you?"

"Yes. Of course. Nothing is perfect. That's why I'm afraid of the government. They want to hire five percent guys to help with economic indicators and crime. But no one is one hundred percent. I don't want to be the one that says that guy killed his wife because he likes killing. What if I'm wrong? The other day I almost didn't recognize my own father. Sure, it's been over twenty years, but still, his face was ingrained in my head. I saw him turn around and his deviated septum had been fixed and his hair had thinned and darkened with age. His voice gave it away."

The aroma hits the table before the food. Coop's brisket sandwiches drip with juice and a heavenly smell of honey, molasses, and pepper. With the sandwiches, he serves baked beans and grilled peaches.

Sammy and Shelly are enjoying the award-winning BBQ meal. Coop cannot pull himself away from his phone to enjoy the meal or the company. His video alerts keep dinging. Shelly calls him on his rudeness, "Coop, what the hell? The food is great but get your ass off your phone. I want to get to know you."

"Two men just popped up outside where Natalie was staying in Lincoln Park. The same two men appeared at the library and coffee shop where I researched Natalie's company."

The inquisitive looks from his guests are followed up by Sammy, "That is some James Bond shit. You have cameras set up around the city? Anything upstairs?"

"I set up tiny cameras at a few locations. I use this face matching program; if the same face appears at more than one location, I get buzzed. Sorry to be rude, but why don't you guys head to Shelly's."

Before she can ask any questions, Coop adds, "Shelly, it's fine. Really. These men have no idea about me. I never met Karen, Natalie's friend. I'm going to find them."

SUN'S OUT

Natalie sits patiently at the Beach Hotel in Byron Bay, Australia. Sydney was amazing, but the big city made her nervous. Walking around the zoo, she felt like the animals and people were watching her. The small surf town she's in now feels safer. The people are all extremely welcoming. While lying at the beach, two topless girls invite her for drinks. Sensing they are good people, Natalie agrees to meet them.

Even though the summer is coming to an end down under, it's still beach weather. Trying to follow Coop's advice, she's reading a book on martial arts, and her company is a bottle of red wine. The hardest part of her trip so far is not checking her email. The one time she got online, she read about Mary Stern's death. Guilt eats away at her, but she knows attending the funeral would've been bad.

Gazing out the window at the beautiful blue water, Natalie feels that leaving the U.S. is the best decision she's made in years. Breathing in the salty air is interrupted by her new friends, Amy and Olivia. They are from Sydney and are on, as they put it, "holiday."

Amy, standing a foot taller than Olivia, puts her arm around Natalie like an old friend would. Before Natalie can stand up from the barstool, Amy is next to her with a hug, "So glad you are joining us!"

Exiting the embrace, Natalie can feel the genuineness radiate off both girls. Sitting down, Olivia scoots her chair close, "What's your story, Natalie? You ready to get drunk?"

Smiling, "Maybe. It's been a long few months. I quit my job, did some traveling in the States, and here I am. It's amazing here. What are your stories?"

Pulling back her shoulder length hair from her face, Olivia answers first. "We both work in advertising in Sydney. We started about six months ago and went through training together with four other new hires. We are the only two still at the company. I don't know if we are tough or stupid. We work a lot."

With a mischievous smile, Amy adds, "Byron is the perfect place to relax, have some drinks and maybe hook up with a boy from another country."

All Natalie can think about is Coop. She's never felt such a connection with anyone. Can you fall in love that fast? She tells herself that it's more infatuation at this stage.

Interrupting her thoughts, Amy asks, "You got a boyfriend? You're too pretty to be single."

The combination of the wine and compliments makes Natalie blush. "Well, I met a man before I left. He has this incredible ability to make me a complete mess."

Olivia comments, "Girl, you really like this guy! You totally slept with him."

With a guilty smile, "No comment. You ladies have a type. I can be a good wingman."

The conversation effortlessly flows as the bar gets crowded. Glancing at the menu, the three women order fries, fish tacos and a Margherita pizza.

Olivia and Amy reapply lipstick while Natalie scans the surroundings. She only senses warmth, while Olivia focuses on men. She waves over a handsome man with a baby face. His face lights up, and he offers up the brightest smile and hug. With an American accent, "Hey Olivia, thanks for inviting me to meet you guys here. Who's this?"

Speaking for Natalie, Amy answers, "This is our new best friend, Natalie. Natalie, this is Olivia's new boyfriend, Mike."

Mike's cheeks turn a deep red; he extends a muscular arm and shakes Natalie's hand. "Nice to meet you. Where are you from?"

Not wanting to explain, "I'm from the US. Sort of all over, you?"

Pulling a chair to the table, "I'm from Milwaukee. I came here for a wedding two weeks ago and just can't get myself to leave."

Amy cuts in, "Well, now that he's met the beautiful Olivia, he might never leave." As Mike accidentally brushes next to Natalie, she senses his euphoria. He really likes Oliva. Curious if she feels the same way, Natalie stands up and puts her hand on Olivia. With all the heat she's giving off, the feeling is mutual.

Annoyed by her friend, "Amy, don't pressure my new boyfriend." Turning to face Natalie, "Mike saw us on the beach, and he actually looked us straight in the eye. Now I don't have the biggest boobs, but Amy does. I was very impressed with his focus."

Laughing feels therapeutic. Getting lost in conversation is something Natalie has not done in a long time. Letting go of worry and enjoying the company takes Natalie out of her funk. Her only sad thought—she wishes Coop was here to share this moment.

INVESTIGATORS

Karen answers the door when two gentlemen dressed in suits knock loudly. "FBI. Please open up, Karen."

Very freaked out, Karen opens the door. Without asking for any proof, she stands at the door in shock. Her profound voice takes the men by surprise. She bellows, "What can I do for you?"

The tall and bald agent, Nalish, speaks first, "We are looking for a young lady that went to college with you. We believe she is in Chicago and may be able to help us. When did you last see Natalie Burns? "

Without flinching, "A few days ago. She was staying with me. She asked to crash a few days before some big vacation. She told me she wanted to get out of the country."

Frustration boils over in the short and stocky agent, Paulinko, "Are you sure? Can we come in?"

Karen's lawyer side comes out, "Sorry, gentlemen. No warrant, I can't let you in. Come back with a warrant, and I am more than happy to oblige."

The taller agent smiles and then kicks Karen in the stomach. All the wind escapes her chest. Her head hits the floor and both men walk in. Paulinko drags Karen's unconscious body into her bedroom. Both men search the apartment with gloves on. Nalish looks through the browsing history on Karen's computer as Paulinko searches every square inch of the apartment. Finding an international phone number in the garbage, the shorter agent dials the number on Karen's home phone. "Hello mate, Sydney tours at your service."

"Nalish, she's in Australia. Dial in."

Sensing trouble, Coop calls the cops. "Police, there's been a break-in at twelve twenty-six Lincoln Avenue. I just saw two men force themselves inside." Since he was already walking there, Coop starts running to Karen's apartment. Shaking his head, Coop fears he will not make it in time to save Karen. Sirens blaze by Coop but it's too late. He sees two men hopping into a Ford Fiesta rental car that was parked in Karen's alley. Trying to read their minds, he keeps running toward their car. With the usual heavy Lincoln Park traffic, Coop reaches the car as they stop at an intersection. Gazing through the shorter agent's mind, Coop picks up Australia. They know. A phone number pops in his mind, and Coop does his trick to remember the digits.

Coop knocks hard on the window. Paulinko rolls down the window, and his foreign accent pops out: "What the fuck you looking at?"

All the years of practice, all the anger towards his father is balled up in one punch: a quick, back-handed crack to the nose. Coop knows that without medical attention this guy will not live. Paulinko's nose is starting to pierce his brain and he passes out. Nalish, the calmer spy, quickly rolls up the window on his side. It's too late. Coop has busted the window and is holding a gun up to Nalish's perfectly shaved head.

"You have thirty seconds to answer this question: Who are you? And what do you want?"

"Listen, you don't want this. Leave, forget me. We are hired spies for our country. We need answers your girlfriend can tell us. She made a few too many bad deals in our country. Even if you kill me, they will find her." Trying to read Nalish's mind, it's black, which means he's trained to think of nothing during crisis situations.

Only moving the gun a few inches back, Coop jams the side of it into Nalish's temple. His head hits the dashboard as Coop quickly grabs wallets and cell phones. Before speed walking away from the mess, Coop places the gun in Paulinko's hand. Quickly ducking into an alley, Coop heads to a club hidden on Armitage Avenue. His heart is pounding through his white shirt as he washes the blood from his swollen knuckles. Taking three deep breaths he tries to relax. All the training that seemed like a game as a child is coming back to him. Slowing down his thoughts, he knows he needs three things:

- *A phone*
- *Five minutes to scan Nalish's phone*
- *An alibi*

Working out of order, Coop looks through Nalish's phone. Mentally taking notes, Nalish visited New York. He's probably been after Natalie for weeks. He only has first names in his phone, with the last names' initials. The majority of his text messages are from 555-718-2463. Coop programs that number in his phone with the name Master P.

Walking toward the doors at the front of the bar, Coop bumps a young kid and swaps phones. "Sorry, dude." As the young man walks off, Coop dials the number he visualized first.

After a long wait, the phone starts to send the call, "Hello mate, Sydney tours at your service." After getting an address, Coop hangs up frantic. They are coming for Natalie.

A striking, intoxicated and horny blond asks, "Are you okay? You look sad."

Using her breasts to cheer up Coop, she leans into him, "Why are you so blue?"

Faking a smile, "I'm Jay Cooper and I hate to be a party pooper."

"You are silly, Jay Cooper." Still not offering up her name, which Coop already knows is Lena, she sits on the chair next to his. "If you guess my name, I'll buy you a drink."

"It's not Nina, Gina, or Rena, but maybe Lena?"

Looking as if she won the lottery, "OMFG! How did you do that? That's amazing! Am I so drunk that I'm about to go home with Dr. Suess?"

Laughing and feeling a little less intense, Coop brushes Lena's hair behind her ear. Her blue eyes sparkle as she smiles. For a moment, Coop loses himself in her beauty. Lena orders two shots of Patron, and Coop thinks it's going to be difficult not to fuck her. "Thank you, Lena. This night is starting to look pretty amazing."

As Lena falls into Coop's bed, he heads to the couch. Natalie is not his girlfriend but sleeping with Lena feels wrong. Heading back to his bedroom, Lena looks angelic. Coop hops in bed and drifts off next to his alibi.

VISITORS

Lena's alcohol-induced sleep prevents her from hearing rapid knocking at Coop's door. Despite the peer pressure from Lena, Coop only drank two shots. He feels well rested. Before opening the door, Coop looks through the peephole. Two CIA agents are standing next to each other with beady eyes scanning the hallway as if a bad guy was hidden between the wood slats.

"Mr. Cooper, please open up."

The door opens slowly, Coop concentrates on their thoughts. They want to know about Fred Smith. Standing in the doorway, Coop deepens his voice. "How can I help you?"

"You are in no trouble. We would like to ask you a few questions about Fred Smith." Flashing their badges, Coop waves them in. Lena pops out of Jay's bedroom in a white shirt and nothing else. The agents try not to stare at her nipples that poke through the shirt as if they are pointing at the gentlemen to leave.

With a yawn, "You need me to leave, Jay?"

Shaking his head no, "No, babe. Why don't you lie back down. I'll bring you some breakfast when my friends leave."

Coop turns on a burner and starts to make oatmeal the old-fashioned way, with milk, on the stove. "You guys want anything? Come on, the coffee literally just buzzed."

The fat and graying agent motions okay and speaks, using his inside voice. "I'll take a cup. I'm Agent Rich and this is Agent Adams. You're pretty calm for having two CIA agents in your house."

"If you wake up next to Lena, even if you committed a crime, you'd be pretty happy right about now. And I'm trying not to freak her out. What do you need?"

"Fred Smith has been poking around your neighborhood. We know Sam, your upstairs neighbor, who has been MIA the past several days, entered a bracket online. Fred works for the company and our guess; he wants to talk to Sam and possibly you. His company is notorious for gambling abuse, physical abuse, and God knows what else."

Agent Rich drones on as Coop continues to make oatmeal and occasionally looks up to show he's listening. Serving both agents a bowl of oatmeal with brown sugar and butter, Coop starts to feel paranoid. Who knows, maybe he's a little freaked out that his father supposedly works with these guys and the mob. These guys clearly don't trust Fred. It's like they're trying to make sure Fred hasn't blown his cover.

Agent Adams finally cuts in, also using a hushed tone. "Last night a woman was attacked in Lincoln Park. The cops found a guy holding a gun, dead, and his buddy is in the ICU. We have no idea if this is related, but wherever Fred Smith goes, a shit storm follows. If you see him, call us."

"He stopped by two days ago. Said something about making sure we didn't cheat. Told us we seemed honest. He left, and I haven't seen him since. I've seen a lot of movies, so this might sound stupid, but I have a trip planned overseas. I don't need to stay put, do I?"

Adams smiles while answering the question, "No, Mr. Cooper. We just want to warn you and hope you'll cooperate."

The smells of cinnamon, sugar, and oatmeal fill Coop's apartment. Lena yells out, "Smells great, Jay!"

As the agents walk out, Rich yells to Lena, "When did you meet Jay?"

Yelling back, "Don't judge me—last night. It was consensual; can he come back now?" Both agents laugh as they leave the apartment.

The moment the door closes, Lena pops into Jay's kitchen. "What the hell? Those were not your friends. Are you some sort of criminal?" Coop can tell that Lena is very freaked out. With a warm smile, he reassures her all is okay.

While serving her breakfast, "It's a long story. The short version: My friend and I entered a March Madness contest online. We are doing well, so we are getting a lot of visitors. My suggestion to you: Never bet on a large scale."

Feeling slightly relieved, "Coop, you really listen. Man, when I said I wanted oatmeal old school, you delivered."

With a smile, "I was not lying when I said I can make some serious oatmeal. My mom taught me to mix in half milk, half coconut milk and it just tastes right."

With a dirty, glance, "Whatever happened last night, I could not tell you, but I would do it all again for one more serving. Is it weird that this makes me feel pretty?"

"Oh, that's just the crystal meth talking."

Shaking her head, "Such a comedian. Can you drive me home?"

Trying not to stare at her breasts is like trying not to look at an accident. Fighting the sex urge, Jay debates if Natalie is his girlfriend. He only saw her a few times, but it's who he really wants. Lena sees the conflict in Jay's eyes, "Relax Coop, I'm not going to rape you. If you bake for me, then it might be a different story."

Looking at the cameras, Coop notices a man standing outside his garage and another man across the street, sitting on a rock, reading a paper. No one sits on rocks. Behind the rock guy, there's a bald man sleeping in his car with the window slightly cracked. "Who do you work for, Lena? Were you paid extra to come home with me?" Trying to read her mind, Coop does not get much. Only that she really wants more food.

"Like your visitors this morning, I'm looking for Fred Smith. He quit after seeing you the other day. Well technically, he said he needed a break. I was looking for him last night. He likes to drink, and we tracked his old cell phone to the club where you and I met.

They send me in because gifted people can't read my mind. Probably because there's not much in there. Oh, and he likes blondes."

Stepping on the deck, Jay notices that the window is now almost all the way down in the car belonging to the old guy. He flashes back to his youth.

His mom's new favorite game is guess the number. She thinks of a number in her head and Jay must guess it. Since he always gets the right answer, she orders, "Go outside on the deck; I'm going to close the door." Jay remembers telling his mom that he's not Superman. After a few tries, Jay gets the number, but the sliding glass door needed to be partially open. While playing this game for hours, Jay's dad yells, "Emm, this is crazy! Let's play ball!"

Concentrating on the bald man, Jay can see there's something off about his head. Trying to read his mind, he quickly realizes it's Fred Smith and he's trying to talk to him. "Get the girl out. Get her out. Lead them away. If you get this, drop something. I can't read minds like you."

Kicking a flowerpot over, "Shit. I am a klutz. You need a ride, or do you want your buddies to take you home?"

Walking on the deck confused, Lena recognizes a coworker and walks back. "Jay, before that guy gets antsy, let's go."

"His buddy is outside the garage. Is this going to get violent?" Trying to read her mind again, Jay gets nothing but confusion. "They wouldn't hurt you, would they?"

"Let's not find out."

Walking out the back door, they get in Coop's car, and he starts the car while opening the garage. A young giant is taken by surprise as Jay pins him between his neighbor's garage and his car. Lena is in shock. "Wait here." Coop pops the trunk, then takes a bat out of the backseat. Coop, like a lion stalking his prey, sneaks out of his car and hides in his garage.

The young body builder is yelling out, "Steve, the back, the back." Another man, with a Blackhawks hat, mullet, and arm tattoos sprints back to the alley. Staring at the open trunk, Jay pops out of nowhere and clocks the guy with the bat. Like a pro, Jay drops the guy in his trunk.

The young guy pinned to the old car is visibly scared as Jay approaches. "Why are you outside my house?" Who sent you?"

"I'm looking for Fred Smith. That's all. We wanted to make sure Lena was okay." Reading his mind, Jay sees that Lena was not supposed to stay over, and, like the CIA, no one trusts Fred.

Coop takes a quick swing to the muscle man's hips. "Tell me the truth! Your ribs are next."

Ignoring the pain, "You and your friend are dead after this shit." Only thinking of Sammy, Jay cracks the guy in the ribs. Pain, fear, and trouble breathing all lead to the giant passing out. Lena, scared, remains in the car.

A disguised Fred Smith drives into the alley. "Let's switch cars. I'll ditch the evidence."

Trying to maintain her composure, tears roll down Lena's face. Jay tries to comfort her as they walk to his father's Ford Explorer. "Listen, that guy wants to kidnap me and he's after my friend as well. Whether you knew it or not, they did not only want Fred."

Shaking and trying to fight the tears from pouring, Jay can read her mind now. Lena is thinking that this was a dumb job and she knew it was too good to be true. Lena is also torn as to who is the good guy and who is the bad guy.

With a comforting tone, "Lena, trust me. Those men are bad men. Your boss is not a good guy. You have to say nothing. They will call you. You will tell them you got to my house around midnight and left shortly after." Purposely talking slowly so she will remember, "You left my house and had a late-night snack at The Wiener's Circle, followed by coffee at Up All Night Café. You lost track of time. Three deep breaths."

Lena starts to calm down as her phone buzzes, "Sal, how are you? I'm walking around Lincoln Park. Been doing it for hours. It was gorgeous last night." Listening and taking deep breaths, "I left his house hours ago. Like two a.m. He had no idea about Fred. I lightly prodded. I don't think he's in the five percent. His friend is on vacation. No sign. He said something about Vegas. His friend is feeling lucky. That's all I got. Still a virgin, Sal. Maybe you should've sent Natalie. I'm going home to sleep. This was an adrenaline filled night." She hangs up the phone and takes a few more deep breaths but can't suck in the tears.

Jay's mind immediately explodes. Natalie? His Natalie? Using all his mental effort, Jay scans Lena's mind for an image of Natalie. Anything—hair color, eyes. "Was Natalie a brunette? Tall, dark skin? New Yorker?"

Lena confirms Jay's suspicion. "Yea. She came to town and we found her right away at the casino. She was playing poker and won a few grand. It was odd; she focused on the players more than the cards. I was working cocktail that night. Sal thought something was up. He let her keep the money if she agreed to help him out. Is she the reason you didn't sleep with me?"

Jay's mind starts to race as if he's on the clock to make the next chess move but has no idea what piece to shift. "She split town before I got to know her better. Real sweetheart. At least I thought."

"Wish I could help you. Didn't know her well. Just knew she made some cash. Be careful. Sal is a dangerous man."

SAVING SAMMY

Sammy wakes up from his never-ending date with Shelly as his phone buzzes with an unlisted number.

"Hello?"

With a hushed and serious tone, "Head to the Palwaukee airport. Pack a bag. I'll text you with details. Wait there until the championship game is over. Take Shelly. I'm sending you a car."

Without letting Sammy get a word in, Jay hangs up. Calling his car service, he sets up transportation. The next step, getting him a pilot. Nina's ex is a rich trader that has a plane usually parked at that airport. He's one of those guys that's so rich he has no idea what to spend his money on. Jay always refers to Rob Snyder as Mr. Good Life or MGL. He was an offensive lineman in college and tapping into his competitive streak he figured out how to make boat loads of money on the computer and trading floor. And even though he looks like a pro-wrestler, he's super nice. Sam also knows him from flag football. "Hey, MGL! How are you?" Without waiting for a response, "Remember that promise about giving me a ride. Well, I need to cash in on that favor. I have two friends I want to surprise them with a trip anywhere you're headed this weekend. It's my buddy Sam and his girl."

"Jay, old man, thanks for the email a few weeks back. I made a quick five thousand on your tip. I can take your friends anywhere. Just got the plane cleaned and gassed up."

"How about the championship game?"

MGL pauses to think it over, "My girl and I were talking about going to St. Louis. I already have tickets to the games."

Jay quickly decides that heading to where the championship game is held, would be the last place the mob would look for Sammy. Who would be dumb enough to go there? "Perfect. I love you MGL!"

"Love you, too! Text me Sammy's number and I'll give him the details."

In the meantime, Sammy tries to play it cool. His smile is a little bigger than usual, and Shelly tries to calm him down. Placing her hand on his shoulder, "I am so excited. This is going to be a great adventure. I've never been on a private jet. I feel like a rock star."

VACATION-ISH

Australia is beautiful. Blue skies and 75 degrees every day. Natalie is trying to enjoy herself, but she cannot help but wonder what's going on in Chicago and New York. Reading the police blotter section, she immediately covers her face, controlling her emotions; no tears drop. Her heart races as she reads about her friend's place being broken into. Two men caught. One dead, the other alive but severely concussed. The dead man is Albanian. That's who's after her. Tageo Corp. She interviewed their CEO and despite an amazing outlook, she recommended her firm pull out of the company immediately. Losing millions of dollars hurts a bio-tech start up, and that's why they are after her. Using a recently purchased phone, she texts Jay, "Tageo Corp."

Without too much mental digging, Natalie remembers the CEO was arrogant, empty inside, and only cared about money and power. Granted, she only met him for two minutes while touring their facility; but she knew he was bad news right away. Even her boss commented on his smirk after he commented, "They sent two ladies. Smart." And then he winked.

Their product line was impressive; they were cornering the market on smart drugs. And researching the benefits of peptides for other governments was a great strategy. The COO, Marcus, was convinced the supplement he was taking cured his gut issues and regrew his hair.

Jotting down all the notes on Tageo that she could remember fills a smart notebook that fits in her bag. Writing felt cathartic. Knowing the enemy also put Natalie at ease. As a research geek, Natalie wanted to sit at a computer for hours and look through their website and social media posts, but that might help them locate her.

Instead of directly researching the company, she pulls up PubMed and reviews all the trials she can find on their drugs.

OLD NEIGHBORHOOD

Jay has no idea what to do now that Lena is gone, Sammy is on a plane, and Fred has his car. The only place he can think to go is his old house.

Driving around his childhood neighborhood, nostalgia fills his mind. The park on the corner is where he got in his first fight. Eddie Charles, this strong-as-nails bully, threw his best friend Josh on the ground. Mild fear and adrenaline unleashed what kids would later call "Crazy Coop." Using his dad's boxing lessons, Coop fired a combo so fast, Eddie couldn't block it. He fell to the ground, hard. His menacing eyes started to wad up with tears. Coop, standing above him, yelled, "You ever touch him or any of us again, and you'll be doing more bleeding than crying." Eddie apologized, but all Coop could think about was his dad. He would've been proud, and the last phrase, he stole from the old man.

Before more memories flow, Coop sees Fred slowly pulling next to him. "Kid, you are good. How did you know to come here?"

Tired and nervous, "Just a guess. I figured my place is not too safe. Although we can check."

Hunched over Jay's phone, the father and son team stare at the different cameras around Coop's house. With his arm naturally over his son's, he can't help but smile. Fred's waited decades for this. It was worth risking his relationship with the mob and his job. Now he just has to explain it to the government.

Rubbing his eyes, "Cops came looking for you this morning. Said they were with the CIA or something. What kind of trouble are you in?"

"I'm a double agent. I help Sal with finding five percent talent, while trying to figure out what his plans are and how to stop it. Except for his penchant for getting guys beat up, it's hard to pin much on him. He's part owner in casinos and clubs. And of course, the contests. We think he has hookers on the payroll, but I haven't seen it."

Jay feels a little better about not having sex with a possible call girl. "Hey old man, how did you know that Natalie was running from Albanians?"

"The government. I went there a few years ago on a fact-finding mission. This one group, they were Nazi like, running crazy tests. Their government condemned the leader, Adrian Shlepski. He went to jail, but his work is still going on. No one has been able to find the lab or the new boss."

With a smile, Coop turns to his dad, "Road trip?"

Without waiting for more information, "Let's go to New York." Coop hands his dad Nalish's wallet, and they search for other clues.

"Old man, Sal is going to keep looking for you. What are you going to do about that?"

"I took his men to your CIA friends from this morning. They spilled the beans on Sal. I couldn't believe how fast. The only problem, Sal will be back on the street in a few hours. He has a few judges on the payroll. However, the press he keeps getting for going to jail will force his partners to freeze him out."

Jay tries to figure out a plan; his perfect life is spinning out of control. The only person helping him is a man he hasn't seen since he was in elementary school. And can you really trust an absentee, alcoholic father? Does he tell Fred about Tageo Corp?

Fred is experiencing pure joy. Despite a bounty on his head and his CIA counter parts no longer trusting him, he's sitting next to the greatest accomplishment of his life. "You still have a great swing, kid."

PRIVATE JET

Shelly and Sammy are drunk before they reach MGL's plane. A good buzz eases Sammy's fear of the mob and calms Shelly's flying anxiety. MGL's ear-to-ear smile also relaxes his passengers. "This will be fun. We'll be there in forty-five."

Shelly grew up with rich friends. She was not rich, but her neighbors were professional athletes, retired surgeons, and savvy investors, but this is her first time on a private plane. "This is impressive, Rob! Thanks for flying us."

Sammy asks, "How did you even think, I'm going to buy a plane?" Shelly, shoots Sam a how-could-you-ask-that look.

Rob responds honestly, "I initially rationalized this purchase by saying, I can see my family any time. But the truth is, I just thought it would be cool to be able to go wherever, whenever. And if Coop keeps giving me tips, I'll have this paid off in no time."

The plane is small, but roomy enough for four people. The luggage compartment tightly fits everyone's bag. Rob seems comfortable behind the controls, and his girlfriend, Penny, knows how to ease first-time flier fears. "Guys, Rob is an excellent pilot! I was a flight attendant for a few years out of college, and no one lands a plane like this guy. Smooth as butter." Offering wine and cheese, Penny plays the hostess role well.

As the plane takes off, Shelly squeezes Sam's forearm. Her nails dig into Sam's skin, possibly breaking a few layers of epidermis. With his other arm around Shelly, he tries to play cool. Internally, he's a mess. Concern over crashing is his last thought. Oddly, that thought settles him down. If the plane goes down, he doesn't have to worry about the mob or what's going on with his best friend.

With moderate wind, the flight is smooth. Rob navigates the sky easily. With a bottle of wine down, Penny and Shelly are happy and chatty. Sam's mind is in reverse. All he can think of is how he never knew Coop was gifted. The guy never studied. Well, maybe 30 minutes before any exam. He wrote papers, term papers, in a few hours' time; it took everyone else days. And the women—he always knew what to say and never forgot a face or name. He would break up with a girl, and she would somehow thank him, as if he just bought her a car.

Sam remembers watching Coop play baseball. He had this beautiful swing but almost always got walked. He saved his best batting performance for the end of games. When Coop was a senior, he homered in the ninth inning of every other game towards the end of the season. Unfortunately, it was not enough to get drafted. Plan B was always the stock market. Coop loved to trade penny stocks. Coop would be up in his room yelling, "I'm going to make this penny a dime, dude!"

ROAD TRIP

Chicago to New York is a 12-hour drive, but sitting next to a man you haven't seen in decades makes it feel infinitely longer. Sports radio and pop music carries the quiet duo to Ohio.

Fred turns off the radio. "I'm sorry, I can't take another Bieber or Taylor Swift song. I like the music but it's like every other song is one of them. What are you thinking about?"

"I'm trying to figure out a plan. We are going to this guy's house. He's alive. His partner is not. He knows Natalie is in Australia. You work for the mob and the CIA. You apparently cleared things up with the CIA, but I'm not totally believing it. What are you thinking about?"

Taking a deep breath, Fred looks out into the dark sky. "I've been a fuckup forever. Then you were born, and the tailspin did not get better. I was a cop, and half my team was dirty. They would beat up a drug dealer, steal his cash, toss him in jail, and then do the same thing to the next guy. This was before cell phones. No cameras sitting in everyone's pockets. Cops could scare people. Sure, there were some great guys, but I didn't want to be around the dirt bags. I started working security at events. I also won a lot of money gambling. The mob started to hate me. You were a baby. My drinking was out of control. I was petrified that the mob would take you and Emma. So, I left. Now I'm thinking, maybe I can right this ship."

Coop, not one to hold back, "I'm hoping you are still not a fuck up." Looking into his father's rugged eyes, he smiles, giving Fred a small window of hope. Focusing back on the road, Coop's magical mind starts forming a to-do list:

- *Check out bad guy's apartment*
- *Capture*
- *Interrogate*
- *Check on Sammy*
- *Fly to Australia*

"Why are you coming with me, Fred?"

"In twenty-six years, I've had visions about you and did jack squat. Now I'm going to help save your life. I can't say it enough: I'm sorry."

Sitting in silence, trying to hold back a smile, Coop appreciates the gesture. All the years of being a drunk plus decades of absenteeism is not forgiven, but it feels good to have someone present. And maybe he can save his father's life. And there is something about Natalie.

Coop turns off the booming voice of Jon Bon Jovi. "Do you hear that? There's, like, something vibrating in the car. Reach under your seat."

Pulling a cell phone out, Fred reads the text messages. "You are being followed. Erase this. Ditch the phone. Reply. Please reply. Seriously reply."

Coop turns to his father, "Fuck. Reply thanks and delete the text. It's the black Honda Accord. It's been a few cars back for miles."

Fred opens up the window and tosses the phone at a boat being pulled by a Ford pickup. Coop's heart races as the phone sails into the boat. "Good shot, old man. They probably know the car. I'll speed up and then we'll switch cars."

As the sky darkens, Coop turns on his Waze app, checks for cops, and then buries the pedal to the ground. The muscle car shoots ahead. Weaving in between the light traffic, the black car is nowhere to be found. Coop is laser-focused on driving—which, at over 120 miles per hour, is a good thing. Fred's huge smile confirms Coop's memory. "You're still crazy."

"Just enjoying some bonding time with my son, Mario Andretti."

Coop, trying to figure out the mystery phone and text, "Who texted you? Lena?"

With a smile, Fred responds, "Probably. She's pretty hot, right?"

"She's alright."

Following the signs to Ohio, Coop figures they can hide the car there and get a rental for the rest of the journey. It will be nice to get some rest and think of a more cohesive plan.

DOWN UNDER

Natalie is making her way up the Great Barrier Reef. The weather is gorgeous, and the people are incredibly nice. She buries fear deep in her belly and pretends uncertainty about her future is just a game. Every room/beach/shop she walks in, she scans for trouble. Once the coast is clear, she starts drinking, playing water sports, and napping.

Growing up with poor parents that bickered constantly was not ideal for someone who could read emotions. Natalie learned how to avoid her own feelings and the important lesson that sometimes, people just want to be sad. Excelling at learning helped Natalie escape her screaming parents that often wished they had never met, let alone procreated. An academic scholarship and new friends introduced Natalie to a new world. Her dream was to study abroad in Australia, and now she's making that happen. Using her camera like a sponge, she is absorbing the sites and capturing each moment to hopefully share with Coop.

She tries hard to not think about him, but there's a point each day that she googles Coop and smiles while staring at him in his baseball uniform.

Coop thinks about Natalie as well. He knows it's crazy to solve a mystery for a girl he just met, and who might have mob ties. As much as he thinks about her, helping his dad is the main reason he's on this crazy journey. Thinking about Fred used to cause a pain deep in his stomach. As awesome of a mom as Emma was, it could never make up for the void of not having a dad. She worked so hard to teach him how to stand at the plate and follow through on his swing, but she was just repeating what Fred said almost every single morning. Like his dad, Coop was an early riser. At four years old, he and his dad would play catch just as the sun came up.

"Old man, you remember playing catch at five a.m.? Did I wake you?"

With a smile, "You were so cute. You would wake up, and with a loud whisper, you would say, 'Daddy, daddy, daddy, are you up?' Finally, I would get up and off we went to play catch or run the bases. We would get so sweaty that mom would make us take a shower. And you loved to shower."

Years of resentment begin to slowly melt away as Coop remembers how his dad always took him in the shower and then pretended to shave him.

As Coop lies down in his bed, he asks the old man a silly question: "How did you shave me all the time and never once cut my face? You always had some toilet paper stuck on your jawline."

"Coop, I used the back of the razor silly. You need to learn these things. Of course, I learned all of it by trial and error."

DUCT TAPE AND BINDER CLIPS

Reaching New York City was easy; finding parking is another story. After circling the building listed for Nalish several times, Coop parks near a fire hydrant. Before getting out of the car, Coop turns to his dad, "He's dead. Someone is in his apartment. If I had to guess, someone is waiting for us."

A smile forms on Fred's face, because he's crazy and loves a good fight. "Let's do this!"

With a disapproving look, "We need a plan; they probably have guns and other weapons."

Pulling out a 100-dollar bill, Fred approaches a pizza delivery guy. "I want your jacket and two pizzas." The business exchange happens quickly. Opening one box, Fred takes a bite, "Want a piece? We now have a plan. You go in the front with the food. I'll pop in through the back window. Three people max."

Internally, Coop is freaking out. He can feel his left eye twitch. Taking deep breaths, he tries to calm down. Sweat starts to drip down from his armpits onto his sides. The gross feeling is quickly discarded as grown men argue whether to take someone else's pizza. Coop can hear a man—with an accent so thick it might be able to cut the pizza—yell, "Hold on, pizza guy. How much?"

Without thinking, "Thirty for the two pies." The door opens quickly, Coop steps in and scans the back window. Like a pro, he distracts the men as his dad pops inside without making a noise. The three men all crowd Coop. They are staring at the pizza boxes, as if they've never eaten before.

"This smells fucking good!" Before anyone else speaks, Fred is choking the biggest guy, who could play linebacker or be a pro wrestler. Coop tosses the pizzas in another guy's face, and then kicks the third one in the crotch. Grabbing his crotch, the short man drops down in pain. Coop elbows him in the chin and knocks him out. Fred is still trying, holding on to the bald guy's back as if he's trying to ride a wild bull. Before the pizza can hit the floor, Coop punches the other man in his round belly. He doubles over in pain; Coop breaks his nose with a sharp elbow and follows up with a blow to his neck.

Fred is tossed on his back as the large man heaves toward Coop. Coop kicks the man right in the knee; it buckles, and Fred follows up, WWE style, with a chair to the man's back. His chin hits the floor hard; you can hear a pop as his jaw cracks on the ground.

Still smiling, Fred looks at his son, "Teamwork! We have about two minutes before one of these guys gains consciousness. Look for clues."

Opening the zipper on his army coat, Fred pulls out duct tape. Coop looks on curiously as Fred tapes each man's hands, ankles, and eyes. He drags one of the men into the kitchen. Coop searches the apartment for clues. Pulling out empty drawers is not helping.

Fred digs back into his pocket and pulls out binder clips. He places one on each nipple and his capture lets out a scream. Fred unzips the man's pants. "What the fuck are you doing?"

Fred places his foot on the man's stomach. "The next clip goes on your nuts." Turning on his cell phone video, "Talk. Where's Nalish?"

"He's dead. We are looking for clues. Sal is not going to be very happy."

Leading the witness a little, Fred continues, "So you killed Nalish. And now you are trying to figure out what's next? Who hired you?" Adding a little more pressure to the extended belly, the criminal is having trouble breathing.

"Sal. He wants to know why they are so interested in the girl. Come on, I can't breathe."

Not letting off any pressure, "Sal who?"

"Fuck you. Kill me." A little more pressure and he caves, "Sal Montego."

Coop finds notes in the garbage about Australia. Kastric Bardha is scribbled on several notes; either just the first name or the last name is on some printed-out emails. Kastric must be connected to Tageo Corp.

Fred edits his video and sends it on to his CIA counterparts. He yells out, "WE GOT TWO MINUTES."

Running to the car, Coop is clearly freaked out, while Fred is grinning ear to ear. "Drive kid. Wow, you kicked some ASS! All that Kung Fu paid off. You could've taken all three by yourself. Fuck, that was amazing!"

Shaking his head in deep disapproval, "Old man, why did you jump on that guy's back and try to choke him out like that. He flipped you, but he also could've fallen back and broke most of your ribs. And duct tape and nipple clips? Who are you?"

"First off, if I can get him unconscious without breaking a leg, busting a nose or other harm, it looks better in court. Sure, your elbow to the chin was perfection, but I'm trying to do minimal damage. And they were Sal's guys. Sal is now interested in your girlfriend."

Driving to the airport, Coop scans for the rental return drop off. His mind is working overload, debating whether a trip to Australia or Albania is his next destination site. "You crazy old man, do we go to Australia because both of these gangs are looking for Natalie, or do we head to Albania and take out the assholes that started the mess?"

Without wasting any time, "Let me head to Albania." With a perverse grin," You go down under. I mean, Australia."

Trying to hold back a smile, "You are such a dirty old man. I think you need my help. And I would never think of putting on gloves and then duct taping the bad guys. We still have not discussed the nipple clips."

Fred's smile is 20-plus years of missing his son. Years of worrying that any interaction with Jay would ruin his life, and it faded with one joint fight. This is not the ideal father–son fishing trip, but it was invigorating. A trip to Australia with his son would be life changing, but he can take care of the evil people at Tageo Corp, and Jay can hopefully handle the rest. Sal, for the moment, is almost behind bars for a long time, and the video he took proves he's still involved in illegal activities. If he can survive a trip to Eastern Europe, he can survive anything.

"Fred, you can't go alone. Not happening." Reading his dad's thoughts, "You are not going to give me the slip at the airport."

With a serious look, Fred says, "You can fight, you can piece together clues, but this is serious. I got this. I have contacts. I'm going to break some laws; take some liberties with a CIA badge I shouldn't even have."

With a look of concentration, "Who is Kastric Bardha?"

Fred's face goes pale. "Fuck. Why didn't I put that together? He sells bombs to terrorists. He's been hiding out for years. He's like Hitler; he collects five percent geniuses, runs tests on them, and murders the ones that don't help him. Horribly deranged psychopaths buy his weapons. I wish you could run away, but we have to fix this because they will come for you."

Staring into Fred's thoughts, Coop sees fear and redemption. "Okay Rambo, you think you can head into a war zone, capture an international criminal and then be cool with the CIA?"

With a smile, "Yup. I'll need your help. Your girlfriend traveled to Albania several times. She might have some intel. We are going to get pre-paid international phones. Only pick up for me. And don't call anyone but me. I want to give you a few tips. People are looking for this girl, both mob and Kastric's people. Get some pepper spray and maybe a baton that retracts. Not sure of the laws there, but get some legal weapons. Binder clips work, and they don't leave a huge mark. Find the girl, hide, then call me. Deal?"

Taking all the craziness in, "Fred, don't die on me."

An embrace surprises Fred. Coop squeezes his father tight. A tear quickly races down Fred's face. This feels like when Coop was four and he would try to hug Fred until he tickled him off. He still remembers the mornings when Coop was little, and he would run out of bed and hop onto his dad's chest. Coop remembers it too; his mom was always so serious, and Fred was a goof that didn't mind. "Your beard is somehow coarser than it was back in the day." Staring into Coop's eyes, Fred's thinking the real redemption is not about his job, but regaining his kid's trust.

HOOPS

Sammy and Shelly are having a great time watching basketball. They are still hanging out with Mr. Good Life, who will not let them pay for anything. The banter and chemistry between Sammy and Shelly is obvious, even to the oblivious MGL.

Sammy is not unattractive or dull, but dating has always been hard for him. He has this small-town charm; it's like he grew up with Wally and the Beaver. If Shelly had to pick one characteristic she likes most, it would be how easy it is to get him to belly laugh. And Shelly is unlike any girl Sam's ever met. She tells dirty jokes like old school Eddy Murphy. Shelly has no qualms discussing her love of cookies and hatred of salad, and she legitimately has cover girl hair. When Shelly catches Sammy staring at her hair, "It's body and bounce. I have no idea how or why the hair gods hooked me up. I would've preferred bigger breasts, for less bounce. Have you heard from Coop?"

Looking at his phone, Sammy wishes he could sense how Coop was doing. Coop, on the other hand, is happy as he visualizes Sammy and the gang having fun.

The weather in St. Louis is horrible, but the hotel is warm and has a great restaurant. MGL made reservations for the three of them. His girlfriend, Penny, has dinner with her parents. Telling a white lie, MGL said he promised his friends Kansas City barbeque.

Sam's nervousness has subsided since he walked off the small plane. His two teams are playing each other in the finals. The best player on the team he picked to win is badly hobbled. And they will probably lose tonight, meaning the mob will not come looking for him.

Shelly has no idea the severity of the situation. She thinks MGL is nice but is worried that Coop is not well. In her short relationship with Sam, Coop normally calls or texts a few times a day. "Sam, is Coop okay? Usually, you two are like sisters."

With a deep breath, "I have no idea if he's okay. That guy is a winner. He finds ways to get out of bad situations. He also happens to be a meticulous planner. His underwear drawer is organized."

"That's weird. Not sure that makes me feel better about him."

Taking Shelly's petite hand in his, "He'll be okay. It might be radio silence for a while, but he's going to be okay."

Feeling slightly better, Shelly slips into a tight black blouse and a short red skirt. "Your legs—hell, everything—looks amazing. I'm going to have to fight the stares off you."

With a kiss on the cheek, "You're sweet, Sammy."

MGL is excited he does not have to spend an evening with Penny's parents. The few times he's met them, it's been a one-way competition with her father, debating who has nicer things. MGL couldn't care less about Porsches (although he has one), vacation homes, or celebrity friends. Unlike Mr. Harrington, MGL survived on ramen noodles and frozen pizza until he figured out how to make money trading. His money was a combination of hard work, studying, and luck. And he's not one to brag. If it wasn't for a mentor, Coop's advice, and others, he would've never been able to buy a plane. Mr. Harrington's only struggle was who to work for, daddy or his father-in-law. MGL even jokes with his girlfriend that the only reason the Harringtons stay together is the power of their joint bank account.

MGL forces his eyes not to pop out of his head when Shelly walks by. "Damn! Sammy is one lucky SOB. You look amazing!"

With a straight face, "I don't care if you have your own plane; we are not doing a three way."

"Girlfriend swap?"

Shelly, still not breaking character, "Come on? No way Sammy can afford her."

MGL agreeing, "True! We have reservations at two places. The hotel, or this fun BBQ place where you are going to get ogled and probably feel uncomfortable, but the food is awesome. Penny will meet us for dessert later. You pick."

Staring at his phone, Sam utters under his breath, "Fuck!" The hobbled player's pre-workout went well and, just like that, goosebumps form on Sam's arm.

Pointing at MGL, Shelly answers, "I choose ogling and BBQ. Not because I want the attention; I just love brisket."

DOWN UNDER

A few days ago, Coop wanted his dad dead. Now he can't take the thought of it. Sure, the man is deranged, unstable, addicted to adrenaline, and possibly high at this very moment, but it's nice having a dad. Trying to put his emotions aside, Coop concentrates and realizes the old man's travel plans are right.

Sal definitely wants Natalie to join his team and god knows what Tageo wants to do. And now Coop is on their radar, along with his dad. "Alright old man, you win. I'll go to Australia, and you head to Europe."

Sitting in the rental car place, Fred pulls out two debit cards. "This is how we track each other. Go online every few days and check the activity. Charge meals, get cash, or buy a shirt every few days. When you take out cash, two hundred, four hundred, six hundred means it's all good. But the odd amounts—one hundred or three hundred—are trouble. If you can't get online, hit up an ATM for past transactions. Five days with no transactions or two odd transactions, the other person flies out to help. Make sense?"

Fred uses his CIA badge to get him through security. Coop watches as the guards don't even look at his dad's bag. Fred waves Coop through.

Impressed with Fred's simple system, "Smart, simple. How am I going to remember the log-in codes?"

"Can you remember your birth year and your mom's? That's the code on-line, username is mustang. And one last thing, at each hotel you are Bobby Brady and I am Greg."

The final boarding call for Coop's flight is announced. Dad and son embrace, Fred holds back the tears. "Good luck Bobby Brady. You need me, you know what to do. Take my backpack. Don't open it up until you are out of the airport in Sydney. No peaking or you'll get thrown in jail. Just read my mind, I know it's killing you. I know you're some kind of Ninja, but the element of surprise is key."

Looking into Fred's thoughts, Coop gets a list:

- *Two electric shock guns and charger*
- *$10,000 in cash*
- *Expandable baton*
- *Duct tape*
- *Watch with built-in alarm*
- *Granola bars*
- *Watermelon Big League Chew*

A smile forms on Coop's face, "How did you remember?"

Fred smiles back, "How could I forget? You were obsessed with that stuff, but only watermelon flavor. Your mom and I worried that you would choke, because you stuffed so much in at once. The cash seems obscene, but you can also deposit even amounts, or buy clothes or guns, and cash helps. And you have no luggage, so buy a suitcase. And if you need a favor, cash is king."

Boarding the plane, Coop remembers how excited he was the very first time his dad gave him the gum. They were finishing up baseball drills, and Coop's reward for running the bases was this magical pouch of gum. He was dead tired; Fred made him round the bases one more time for unlimited gum access. His mom rarely allowed gum, and Coop could not wait to take full advantage.

Taking his seat, Coop tries to rest. Too bad his dad didn't put an iPad in the bag.

SEARCH BEGINS

Landing in Sydney slowly wakes up Coop. With no idea where to start his search for Natalie, Coop buys a guide on Australia, complete with maps and the best route to take when heading to the Great Barrier Reef. Since he's traveling with a baton and other weapons, trains and busses will probably be the best means of transportation.

The overwhelming feeling of jet lag sets in as Coop eats a delicious lamb wrap in Darling Harbor. Finding the closest hotel, Coop crashes for the day and night.

Breakfast at the hotel is delicious—seasonal fruit with yogurt and honey. It tastes like the berries were picked that morning, and the coffee is strong! Coop feels energized to track down Natalie. Of course, there's a feeling of self-doubt. What if this is a set-up, or worse—what if she does not want Coop's help? Either way, Coop scribbles down a plan:

- *Buy clothes and bag*
- *Bus ride to Byron Bay*
- *Short trip to Brisbane (can hold a Koala there)*
- *Brisbane to Rockhampton*
- *Rockhampton to Cairns/Great Barrier Reef*

Basing his trip on buses, trains, and rental cars, it should take about three to four days with lots of driving and little of anything else. He should hopefully find Natalie somewhere along the way. The last time he heard from her, she was in Byron Bay.

ALBANIA, REVISITED

Fred steps off his plane in Greece and immediately is greeted by a lanky man dressed in a gray suit with a black tie. "Fred, I cannot believe you agreed to this."

"I was always going to do the job. Just had to square up Sal first. How are you, Tommy?"

"You are so full of shit. You had a great thing with the mob. Man, all the drugs and hookers you must have fucked. You sober?"

Shaking his head, "I'm sober. Let's get the car, asshole." Walking through the airport quickly, Fred tries to see what's going on in Tommy's head. His ability is not what it used to be; he's a little jealous of his son. Of course, Coop always had stronger skills, but age and booze haven't helped. A few years ago, Fred could take two weeks off drinking and be razor sharp. Hopefully when the jet lag passes, his mind will clear up. Right now, all he sees is an empty room.

Tommy's been in Eastern Europe for two years. His goal is to bring Kastric to justice. They needed someone with Fred's ability to help. "Fred, where are your recruits? I thought working for Sal was going to help the CIA with a team of you freaks to save the world."

"Well, you'll have to settle for me. We'll get this asshole. I know where he's working."

Tommy, intrigued, "Where? And how did you get the info?"

"Tageo Corp. And did you forget, I'm a genius." Tommy shakes his head as they drive off in a Blue BMW.

Tommy stops smiling, "I know you hate briefings, but we have a week to talk, figure out a plan and find this loser. Intel says he's leaving for America soon. He has a team in Australia searching for some girl. They capture her and then meet in the States."

An unusual sensation takes over Fred's body: concern for others. Logging into the computer in front of him, he looks up his credit card and sees the charge at a hotel in Sydney. Without wanting to draw Tommy's attention, he emails the hotel. Thank god, they have an instant messenger tool.

VERY IMPORTANT, LEAVE MESSAGE FOR Bobby Brady: Coworkers in town from EU. They are looking for Cindy and bringing her to US. Gregg.

BEACHES, BOOBS & BAD GUYS

The first few weeks for Natalie were filled with beautiful beaches, fruity drinks, and learning to surf. Every day she woke with no worry, until today. Busses, trains, and a boat trip brought her to Cairns. Her plan to meet Coop at The Great Barrier Reef is iffy; she needs another plan—stat.

Coop, although stressed since receiving his dad's message, is enjoying the current view. His bus just arrived at Byron Bay. Using his dad's debit card, Coop has no problem finding a quality hotel. Aaman & Cinta Luxury Guesthouse & Villas will offer a great night's sleep before the next leg of his journey. Because the last time he heard from Natalie was from this town, he scans the entire island. The sleepy little tourist spot is filled with beautiful beaches.

Walking down a topless beach is much harder for Coop than he thought. Most of the girls are young and attractive. Consciously trying not to stare at boobs, Coop makes his first friend. She's sitting alone and waves to Coop. "Hi, I'm Jenny. You can remember Jenny from Germany. I haven't seen you around the beach."

Sitting down next to Jenny's tan body, Coop stares into the blue water. "I'm just passing through on my way up the coast. I heard even if it was for a day, I needed to come here. How long you been here?"

Jenny answers quickly, "Two weeks. I can't seem to leave. My friends headed to Brisbane yesterday, and I told them I wanted one more day. It's a short trip." All Coop heard was two weeks; she had to have seen Natalie at some point.

Scanning her memories, Coop sees this girl loves to drink, sleep, and smoke pot. A cloudy mind is usually a difficult one to read. "Have you met a lot of Americans here?"

"A few," As Jenny starts thinking about all the people she's met, Coop senses she's met Natalie. "Not a lot of boys, though. Where are all the American men?"

Flashing his million-dollar smile, "Right here." Catching a glimpse of her huge, tan breasts flusters the usually cool Coop. "What's there to do around here?"

"I met a few nice Australians. Meet us at the Beach Hotel for a drink later. This place is pretty chill; you surf, drink, and smoke. I might never go home."

"Did you by chance meet a brunette, American girl? A little taller than you? She's a good friend; we had a stupid plan to meet in Cairns, but I have no idea if I'll find her."

Coop sees Natalie's face in Jenny's mind as she starts talking, "Sure. She's pretty. Ex finance girl trying to be a writer."

Trying not to seem like a detective, "Yup, that's her. She left New York for a chance to see the world, starting here. My plan to meet her here for a drink might have been a little too romantic."

"Not at all. I think it's sweet. You American boys will do anything for the right one. She left a few days ago, probably landed in Cairns by now."

Coop's concern for Natalie starts to build, "Think I would be crazy to drive to Brisbane tonight?"

"The driving here is scary. A lot of one-way roads that people drive both ways on. And it's a long way down some of those crazy turns. Leave in the a.m. Enjoy the night."

Jenny purposely stands up, so Coop can see her curves and test how serious he is about Natalie. "You are just teasing me, Jenny from Germany."

With a wink, "That's what I do. I'll see you tonight."

Trying to figure out his next step, Coop sits at an outside café. Watching three men pop out of a tiny smart car makes him nervous. Who wears jeans with a polo to the beach? They do not fit in. As they walk by, their shirts poke up a little in the back—must be guns. Taking a knife from his table, Coop walks quickly to their car. After puncturing a tire, Coop puts the knife back and runs to his hotel room.

The great thing about cargo shorts, lots of pockets. Placing both electroshock guns in a pocket with some duct tape, Coop heads back out. Part of him wants to hitch hike to the next destination but these guys will be following him the entire time. Maybe this buys him a few more days without hoodlums chasing him.

As the sun starts to drop, Coop sees all three men trying to change their tire. From a distance, Coop reads their minds. They are looking for Natalie, whom they have a picture of and a man. No idea his exact features but the general description is Coop.

Scanning the area, Coop sees no one near the men. This is his chance. The only question, how to subdue the third guy? With one guy on the ground and the other two gazing at the beach, it's an easy decision who to shock first. The two smaller men drop like flies the minute Coop fires the gun. Surprisingly, the men falling does not even faze the large, pale man trying to remove the tire. With no idea how long these men will be out, Coop quickly tapes their hands, eyes, and mouths. Without wasting time for the legs, Coop grabs a handgun from one guy and sneaks up on the third guy.

Looking startled, with a thick accent, "FUCK!"

"Lay on the ground, face down, and whisper." With a quick kick in the knee, Coop repeats, "Whisper—how many more guys are in Australia?"

Reading his partially empty mind, Coop sees no one, despite the man lying, "Six of us. You better shoot me and run."

He can also tell his guy is about to try and stand up to fight. Placing his foot on the man's neck, "Don't even think about it. I want the truth. When will Kastric send more guys?"

Seeing the number three, Coop places his foot on the man's bulging vein in his neck until he's unconscious. Popping the surprisingly large trunk, Coop sees crazy weapons, including grenades. He takes one grenade and closes the trunk. Next up, he rolls two bodies into the backseat. He places the third behind the wheel and puts the car in neutral. Hopping in the passenger side, Coop starts the car and places the unconscious man's foot on the pedal. Tossing the car into drive, Coop jumps out the door. The car heads towards the empty beach. Testing out his old throwing arm, Coop pulls the pin out of the grenade and tosses it into the open trunk.

Walking away as if nothing happened, Coop walks to the Beach Hotel. As Coop steps in the bar, loud music covers the explosion. The only other loud noise is Coop's heart, pounding through his shirt. He takes a few deep breaths, hoping to lower his heart rate. Now, to find someone to drive him towards his next destination.

Despite training his knuckles for punching, a little pain shoots down his arm. It's been almost a decade since his serious martial arts training and some of the nerves must have healed.

Coop has a flashback to college. Prior to this craziness, that was the last time he hit anyone. Some frat guy grabbed his girlfriend's arm and, without even thinking, Coop smacked the guy so hard on the jaw the kid passed out. When two fraternity brothers tried to retaliate, Coop quickly kicked one guy in the ribs and flipped the other over a coffee table. That awful feeling of hurting someone was so bad, Coop promised himself that only in a dire situation would he fight.

SECRET AGENT MAN

Fred has spent the past few days reading up on Kastric and what the team in the EU has done so far. This guy is one crazy son of a bitch. Kastric finds his 5% through poker and finance, and then pays them to recruit friends. Once he discovers someone's strengths, he pushes them to their limit. He's like an evil villain from a comic book, attempting to amass an army for some sinister plot.

Fred's colleagues, Tommy and Brian, are excellent researchers. The intel on this guy is amazing, but for the past two years, they haven't come close to nabbing him. The goal is to shut down his entire organization, find his partner, and then it's on to the next crazy terrorist group. He has countless names and is associated with a lot of companies; now the team is focused on Tageo Corp. "I'm going to start playing some poker."

Tommy shakes his head, "You are not going there. Thanks to you, we know the company he's hiding behind. Let's bring the bait to him. Bring the girl to the EU."

Shaking his head, "You guys and all your fucking plans. Stop the shit. There is one reason you wanted me to come here. I'll find a game. I guarantee you, once I take a bunch of cash, he'll find me."

Brian, who lobbied against Fred's help, jumps in, "Fine. Tommy, you wanted this cowboy to help. Send him out there. Worst case, he ends up killing himself."

With a smirk, "Brian, you're a young, naïve shithead. You got in the program because of nepotism and ass-kissing skills. You've been here for years with zero sightings. However, I appreciate you backing me on this. What you two pencil peckers couldn't do in two years, I'll do in two days."

As Fred walks out of the room, Tommy and Brian are both annoyed but know he's right. Fred has made a career around getting himself in and out of sticky situations. And since he's curbed his drinking, he can already feel his mind growing stronger.

Tommy runs after Fred, "We'll meet you at the gaming district. Let's keep it simple; ear tug is trouble. Your phone is how we track you if you get kidnapped." Handing Fred a watch, "This is also a tracker and a camera. Push the dial to start and stop recording."

"You guys are so James Bond."

There is only one legal gambling casino area in Albania, Regency Casino Tirana. It's a massive facility that follows strict international gambling regulations. With only one place to legally gamble, there are several illegal clubs, but getting in is near impossible for outsiders. Fred figures if he spends a few days making money at various tables, Kastric's henchmen will come for him.

Before heading to the casino, Fred logs on to his bank website. Coop took out $200 this morning; he must be doing okay. The newfound concern for his son pushes Fred to avoid popping into one of the many bars he passes along his journey to Tirana.

The casino is a work of art. The Regency is like the hotels in Vegas, but more elegant. The first thing that catches Fred's eyes are women. They are all perfect, tall, curvy, with dark hair and even darker eyes. While sitting at a Blackjack table, one waitress approaches him and out of all her assets, Fred notices her long eye lashes first. She winks as she speaks perfect English, "Hello. What can I get you, sir?"

"Club soda with a lime. Thank you." Focusing on the table, Fred starts off betting slow. His mental ability allows him to begin counting cards while chatting with the two other men at the table. They are both Israelis taking a short vacation—at least that's their cover.

Ari and Tal have some sort of system. Ari consistently wins, and Tal loses. Tal complains after the last hand, "How are you two so lucky. Fred, maybe you can give me some pointers."

"Kid, I would love to, but your buddy is on fire. Might want to ask him for some help." Throwing the beautiful waitress a tip, Fred follows Ari to the men's room. "Lead the way; this place is a fucking maze."

As they walk to the bathroom, Fred's voice turns into a soft whisper. "You kids have to get out of here. They are going to figure something is up, and the guy upstairs is crazy. Krav Maga won't save you."

Ari grins, his dark skin further accentuating his bright smile. "Maybe we want to meet the man; this is like *The Wizard of Oz.* Maybe he can give my friend card skills and me a heart."

"Kastric is legitimately a sociopath. He's going to capture the three of us and I'm not sure I can help you." Fred has never looked out for anyone since he disappeared from his family; suddenly reconnecting with his son is giving him a heart.

Ari looks at Fred, deep in his eyes like he's reading his mind. With his phone, he types, "IDF. 5%." and hands it to Fred. Fred types back, "CIA. 5%."

Ari's smile grows. He hugs Fred as if they are long-lost friends, and whispers in his ear, "Super Friends, Avengers, we got this!"

Fred whispers back, "I like you, confident kid."

HITCHHIKE

Coop scans the bar for his German friend, Jenny. She spots him first. His worried look throws her off, "Coop, you okay?"

Forcing a smile, "I'm fine but I need to go. I'm worried about Natalie." Trying to figure out how the girl knew he was off puzzles Coop. He wonders, is there blood on his shirt?

"Your right hand is shaking. You need a drink, Coop."

Taking a shot of tequila and a few more deep breaths, Coop settles down. His first order of business is to scan the bar and locate someone with transportation. Preferably, that someone should be sober. "Do any of your friends have a car? I would pay top dollar to head off tonight."

A basketball-tall Australian steps forward, "Mate, I can take you. I'm heading up the coast. I have a buddy that has a seaplane."

Reading the man's mind and adding a hundred dollars, "I'll cover gas and four hundred bucks."

With a smile, "Name is Adam. Leave in five?"

"Call me Coop. I'll get your cash from the ATM and then we roll. Half now, half when we get there?"

"That's fair, mate."

Jenny nods her head in approval as both men look at her for assurance.

"Funny boys, you are both dealing with good mates." With a wink, "Drive safe."

While heading outside, Coop sees fire and rescue cleaning up the mess at the beach. Cops are walking around talking to everyone. Coop heads straight to the ATM and notices his father has taken out a few hundred bucks. Slightly relieved, he takes out $200 and walks quickly to his ride.

Loading his luggage inside Adam's silver Toyota Corolla, Coop finally starts to relax. Adam seems decent; he grew up in Brisbane and knows all the roads well. "Don't get nervous, mate. I use this app Waze—lets me know accidents, cops, and other traffic issues."

As if navigation is making Coop nervous, he smiles, "Good to know."

Taking turns while driving way too fast scares Coop. Straining to use his powers, he picks up minimal traffic, which eases him for the moment.

SUPER FRIENDS

The pit boss approaches Tal, Ari, and Fred as they rack up twenty grand in winnings. Sensing they are in trouble, Fred manages to quickly give back eight. Ari, having tried this before, knows you have to win big to get noticed. He doubles his bet and makes another killing. "I FUCKING LOVE YOU, DEALER!"

Tal watches with amazement. He is not a member of the 5% club but his hands and feet are so quick you would think he was. He is a Krav Maga instructor for the Israeli military and works well with Ari. Having grown up watching Ari win at everything from poker to basketball bets, he knew Ari had a gift. It wasn't until they were captured by Hamas that he learned Ari's mind truly worked on another level. The only nervous man in the room is Fred. His mind sees the three of them getting thrown out and then picked up in a limo.

The pit boss, sharply dressed in a black tuxedo, approaches the dealer at Fred's table. After exchanging whispers, the dealer walks away. "Gentlemen, you have done quite well here. Please take your winnings and leave the casino." Before they can finish gathering their chips, four NFL-sized security guards surround them.

Fred speaks first, "Loud and clear. NO need for force."

The pit boss walks the gentlemen outside, with the jumbo security guards not too far behind. A Lincoln Town Car greets them; Ari whispers in Fred's ear as they step inside the black stretch. "Just follow my lead."

Ari turns to the driver, "Good sir, please take us to the Hyatt."

With a muffled accent, "Okay. Sirs, we visit one stop on way."

Ari quickly types a message and hands his phone to Fred. "He's taking us to meat packing district. No cabs or rides to be had there. This guy, Nash, he reads people, makes sure they are not cops or thieves, then and only then Nash brings the men to Kastric. Or he kills the people. Clear your mind."

Shaking his head no, Fred types back quickly. "They are going to try and kill us. Grind us up and probably serve us."

Ari smiles, deletes the message, and responds, "Possibly."

The black Town Car stops in front of a meat plant. Two men stand at the entrance. With fake smiles and bad English, "Come. We talk." The fatter of the two is bald with a shiny dome. The other man has a handlebar mustache. Both seem genuinely happy when they see Fred.

Fred takes a deep breath; was he just set up? Looking at Ari, "You fucking set me up!"

Ari greets the two men, "Nash, Sven, we brought you what you wanted. I think he will grind up nicely." As the three men walk closer to the door, Ari leans into Fred and whispers, "Look more scared."

The inside of the meat plant smells like bleach until they get outside the meat locker; then it smells awful. The combination of raw meat and bleach makes Tal queasy. Leaning into the closest garbage, he pukes, spits, and then color begins to fill his cheeks again. Sipping water from the drinking fountain, Tal ignores the laughter and sneaks a look around the perimeter. The large facility is relatively empty. The only other exit is 30 yards in front of them. No way Kastric is here.

Nash picks up his old-school Blackberry, "Kas, we got the American."

Fred, no longer acting, "They are going to kill you and Tal."

Before Sven can lift his handgun level with Tal's head, Tal punches him in the throat and twists Sven's arm. Sven's eyes bulge as if they are about to pop out of his head. The gun pops off and all 200 pounds of Sven hit the ground hard. The noise can be heard through the phone. Nash freezes up as the blood flows down the floor.

Ari is now holding a knife to Nash's neck and grabs his balls. Ari softly but firmly states, "Tell Kastric he needs to get the American quickly, as his comrades are tracking him."

Nash follows through. When he hangs up the phone, he turns to Ari, "Kill me."

Like he's asking to use the bathroom in grammar school, Fred shoots his arm in the air. "Wait. If you want us to kill you, tell us a few things, or we deliver you to Kastric as a snitch. Why is he tracking down that girl in Australia?"

"She cost him millions. He knows she has a rare gift. He wants her to make up that money. It's over a hundred million dollars. He wants to study her. Clone her."

Turning to Ari, "Let go of his balls and ask him a question. Unless you're enjoying it."

Ari laughs, "I am enjoying it. These balls are huge! Not really. Okay, where's his home? How many will be with him? Where is Oren?"

"His address, I don't fucking know. He lives on Crosno and Snowdin. Guards everywhere, it's a fortress. He needs to be killed by a sniper or a large gang. Three fucking guys don't stand a chance. Anyway, he will have a driver, and two men with him. I don't know about Oren. Good luck."

Nash reaches into his pocket, pulls out a gun and quickly takes his own life.

Fred looks at his new partners, "Leave. Seriously. Kastric is not picking me up. Whoever does, you follow. Put the cross streets in your phone. I don't think they will take me there, but we don't want to forget. It might be true."

Ari picks up Nash's phone, puts the sim card in his phone, steals his keys, and fires the gun one more time. With a wink at Fred, "See you soon, Super Friend."

PARADISE

The beaches in Australia are picturesque. Natalie's dark skin glows with a sun kissed tan. The combination of nerves, surfing, and boxing lessons are wearing her down. Her weight has dropped and she's worried that next up is hair loss. Trying to enjoy fish tacos, she scans the beach hoping for Coop to save her. Every day she combs the beach like a homeless man with a metal detector. She can sense he's coming but no idea when or where. She wishes they thought this through prior to her leaving.

Coop isn't far behind. As if worrying about Natalie wasn't enough, he's concerned Fred has been captured. He knows Fred is still alive, but things are not going well. Adam senses uneasiness in his passenger.

"What's going on? You okay? A few hours, the sun will come up and we'll be near the plane. It's small in there, so hope you don't get claustrophobic."

With a forced smile, "I'll be okay. Just a little worried for my girl. I never should've let her go alone."

Adam's relaxed Australian accent has a sedative effect on Coop. "You're doing the right thing. Close your eyes; I promise you we are headed in the right direction." Trusting no one, Coop reads Adam's mind every few minutes, and each time, good vibes.

The bright sun glares into Adam's car as Coop wakes up. Turning to his passenger, "Good rest, mate? We'll be there soon. So, you should know, Steve is crazy. He will fly you wherever for a good buck. No idea how much. Ask him to list off the hot spots. He heads down there looking for girls all the time."

With a big yawn, "Thanks, dude. You trust him?"

With a smile, "If he wasn't my cousin, you would get a different answer. He's a fisherman, and it's been slow. So for cash, he'll take good care of you."

Slowing down, Adam points out his cousin. "There's the man. He even looks sober."

Taking one look at Steve, Coop scans his mind. He seems okay. Adam makes the introduction, "Steve, this is my guy Coop. Coop, my cousin—the pilot, pimp and purveyor of Trips and Fish."

After a handshake, Coop comments, "I'm looking for my girlfriend. A beautiful brunette, American. I think she's in Cairns. The truth is, maybe she's somewhere along the way. Natalie is her name."

"I saw one newish face. Dark skin, head always in a book? A little quiet. Tall?"

Shaking his head in amazement, Coop adds, "That's her. She's in some trouble, I need to find her!"

Steve flashes a huge smile, like the Joker, "She's in Cairns. Got there a few days ago. Work has been slow, which makes it flirting season. And this time of year, there are not a ton of Americans here."

Reading Steve's mind, he's telling the truth. And he wants twelve hundred dollars. "Let's cut to the chase—twelve hundred. Cool?"

As Adam drives away with a wave, Steve fires up his boat/plane. Beer cans litter the floor, and two oversized pieces of pizza occupy the co-pilot's seat. Steve flashes this evil/crazy smile, "I'll even throw in some pizza. It's no New York or Chicago style, but it might change your life. Freshest tomatoes ever!"

Eyeing the pizza as if it might be toxic, Coop scans the beach; sure enough, a pizza stand sits a few yards away. Hungry and groggy, Coop digs in.

"For another hundred, I'll take you to all the coffee shops she might be at."

Coop again reads his mind, "There's what, two Starbucks up there? I'll find her. Thanks for the reminder. I forgot how much she loves coffee."

The choppy flight has Coop thanking himself for only eating one piece of pizza.

SHOOTS AND SCORES

Duke is playing Syracuse for the championship. And although Sammy picked Duke to win, he hopes they lose. The hobbled player isn't playing well, but they still have a lot more experience than Syracuse. A number pops up on his phone, he has no idea who it is. Maybe it's Coop? "Sam Linch, this Bobby Shore. I'm with Online Millions. Good luck tonight!"

Sam's heart races, he tries to put on a happy face for Shelly, "Thanks Bobby."

"Sammy, if Duke wins, come on the court right after the game is over. We will let you know if you won. Of course, a lot of people selected Duke but the score, 78–75—that's just you buddy. Win or lose, have fun!"

Trying to enjoy a beer, Sammy takes a few sips. Then he hears Coop's voice in his head, "deep breathes." Shelly leans in and presses her chest warmly into Sammy, "Are you okay?"

"I need Duke to lose. It's a long story but if they win, and I win this tournament, it won't be pretty for me. "

MGL chimes in, "Relax Sammy. I promised Coop I'd take care of you. And Duke is not winning this game. If Ty was healthy different story."

LANDING

Landing on the water is choppy. Coop turns to the side and pukes; immediately he feels relief. Steve chimes in, "Sorry, bud. Happens all the time. When the waves are thrashing like today, nothing you can do but puke. Or Surf."

Trying to earn back his guy card, "I'm fine. Thanks. What coffee shop is my girl's?"

"So now you want to pay?"

Taking the cash from Coop's hand, with a smile, "Walk off this beach, and just keep walking until you have to cross a street. There you go. No idea if she'll be there, but I saw her there a few times. You need any other flights, here's my card."

Coop looks like some sort of weebble wobble toy as he slowly regains his land legs. Before walking off the beach, a Gatorade quenches his thirst. Peeking inside the coffee shop, his heart skips a beat. Natalie is now perfectly tan, with a few highlights in her wavy hair. Her gaze meets his and then she drops her head on the table.

Focusing on her thoughts, he hears her soft voice, "If you can read my mind, knock on your thigh three times." With three knocks, her thoughts continue, "The three men behind me, I think are out for me. Probably some sort of van with a few others. Be careful. And I really missed you."

Pretending he's unsure what to order, Coop scans the room. The three men behind her look out of place, like they are villains from a cop movie in the '80s. There are a few gold chains, gold watches, and the style is completed with socks peering out of their flip flops.

Listening to what little thoughts they have is easy. They want the girl and her friend. They will take them back to the van and bring the girl, alive, to Albania.

Coop walks outside and surveys the scene. Acting like a tourist, he pops into a shop while scanning the street for a van. His gut says white van. "I'll take that hoody with the big pockets. Might put it on now."

The over ambitious Australian adds, "IT'S AWESOME! I keep all my shit in there. Those pockets can hide a lot of pot." His volume drops. "You need some, dude?"

Smiling, "Just the hoody. Thanks, man." Stuffing his stun guns in the pockets, Coop continues to scan the area. He spots a white rental car van with two men sitting in the front.

Slowly approaching the car, Coop notices both men, also wearing gold chains, and they are holding one hand against the car door facing each other. Hoping his ninth-grade science holds true, Coop fires a shot at the door. Twenty thousand volts quickly shake the van, and both men convulse. Looking stunned, but only slightly impaired, the men seem okay. Acting quickly, Coop opens the door and stuns the first guy again. As he falls to the floor, his partner, a startled stocky man, reaches for a gun. Coop's stun gun has one last charge left, and he quickly deploys it while getting punched hard in the jaw. Lucky for him, his victim responds with foam and possible cardiac arrest. Coop struggles to toss both bodies in the back of the truck. After tying up the guys, Jay grabs their guns, keys, and wallets.

Ditching everything but their IDs and a gun, Coop heads back to the coffee shop. His legs carry him faster than planned. How will he take down these three guys? Before stepping inside, Coop sees his pilot. "Hey Steve, you want to make another few bucks?"

Steve smiles, "Anything for you, mate."

"Thanks, head inside the coffee shop. Yell for Natalie and then take her to your boat. There will be three guys not so far behind. I'll take out one of them, and then I might need your help with the other two."

Without any hesitation, "Done." Steve walks in the coffee shop and calls for Natalie. Sensing this is coming from Coop, she bolts out of the café. They speed walk to the boat/plane. The three men slowly get up and pretend they're done drinking coffee and eating muffins. It looks like they should've quit eating muffins a few years ago. Eyeing the area, the men spot Natalie and jog across the street.

Steve watches as the men approach his boat. Before he can say hi, Coop cracks one guy across the head with a boogie board twice. Steve kicks the chubbier of the two in the stomach and the man quickly drops. The last man standing has a gun pointed in his back. Coop yells, "On your knees."

Coop tosses tape to Steve. "Tie up their hands, legs and mouths." As Steve gets to work, Coop almost rips off the bald man's long ear. "Why are you following the girl?"

"My boss wants her alive. You two can die."

With a smile and a whack on the head, "Funny, my boss says you can die."

Coop can only think, this is much easier with help. Steve has a huge grin, "Haven't seen this much action since I was in the Army. I got a few buddies at the police. Where are the others?"

Coop looks at Steve. "Thanks. They are in a white van across the street. And tell them the girl you were helping skipped town."

With a smile, "Oh, I'm going to say we were arguing over you hot stuff. I'm going to wait two hours. That will give you time to catch a flight out of here."

Tossing Steve a few more bucks, "Best money I've ever spent. Thanks for everything."

Natalie's heart beats through her black crop top. This is way more action than she's ever seen. Coop holds her shaky hand as they speedwalk to her hotel.

GAME SCORE

The score of the game is 78–75. Mister Good Life jumps up from his seat screaming, "OH, SHIT!"

Sam looks up at the sky and thanks God that Duke lost. Man, Coop got it wrong, for once. Then again, everyone probably picked Duke to win.

MGL, smiling ear to ear, "Fucking Coop! He called this. He told me the score. That guy is amazing!"

Reading Sam's confusion, "Cut me a break, Sam. I just won fifty thousand from a friend. I'm pumped. Let's celebrate!"

Shelly kisses Sam's sweating head. "You can relax now. Maybe start with a shower."

Sam surveys the scene in disbelief; no one tries to grab him and end his life. Letting out a sigh of relief, Sam asks, "Can we get a drink?" While everyone celebrates, except the Duke fans, Sam can't help but wonder if this was somehow the plan all along. The urge to call Coop takes over, but like the previous four phone calls, no one picks up.

MGL turns to his new friends, "Can we celebrate tonight and fly back in the afternoon? If you want to go home tonight, I'll fly you back first class. Fifty thousand can fly you first class. Or stay with me and Penny and party like ROCK STARS!!!"

Shelly responds for the both of them, "We are in!!! Sammy and I need to get cleaned up. Is that cool?"

MGL, drunk and smiling ear to ear, "Fuck yea! I'll sober up and we'll get drunk together! No more sipping, Sammy. It's slamming time!"

Sam agrees with a relieved smile, "For sure!"

CAPTIVITY

Sitting in the back seat of a Lincoln Town Car feels unnatural for Fred. He's used to crappy bureau cars and SUVs. Kastric sits across from him very comfortably. "It's a nice car. I wanted a Beemer, but this is easier for conversations. Shocked to see me? I figured you killed Nash, and he was like a cousin to me. But that loser killed himself. What a fuck. And your Arab friends—those guys got paid. Now they have to deliver the girl."

In his mind, Fred starts to question his new friends. Arab is much different from Israeli. Those guys were definitely Israeli, right? Fred's other thought: This guy is much shorter than he expected. It's like meeting an actor or something.

Kastric continues to talk, "I will trade you for the girl. When we call the CIA, that's our deal. Or I pay you? I know you don't have a conscience. I bet you can be bought. Five million?"

Fred contemplates the deal. That's a lot of money. And this girl isn't going to be killed, at least not yet. Kastric continues, "Hey, I want the girl and that asshole who's helping her. He can be dead or alive. But I need proof—like his fucking heart!"

Something inside Fred snaps. Without thinking, he elbows the bodyguard next to him and breaks his nose. In no time, Fred grabs the man's gun and shoots him. The brakes pull the car to a halt and the contents shift. The guard that's still alive opens the door and kicks Fred out. He then pops out while Kastric drives away. Firing twice, Fred shoots the bodyguard who falls almost on top of him. Using all his strength, Fred pushes the man's giant frame away.

Trying to spot Kastric and the driver, bullets fly towards Fred. The feeling of blood rushes over him as he hops behind a parked car. Fighting off pain, he hobbles away from the car and drops behind a giant tree. The light from a car blowing up illuminates the sky. A dark van is the only car on the street until an ambulance and firemen fill every inch of the street. Before the rescue workers approach, Fred is plucked inside the van.

With eyes full of blood, Fred uses his mind to see who saved or maybe captured him. Before passing out, Fred utters, "He thinks ... he thinks you two are Arabs."

PART II: PARANOIA

Pulling into the alley, MGL drops off Shelly and Sam. Sam shakes MGL's hand. "Thanks for the ride and the game. Great weekend!"

MGL responds with his million-dollar smile, "Yeah, buddy. Let's do it again. Say hi to Coop for me."

Outside of Sam's building is a for sale sign. The contact person is Nina Gold. Turning to Shelly, "Jay's assistant?"

"I have no idea. I don't know Nina's last name. Call her."

Sam, confused and angry, dials Nina. "Hey Nina, what's up with the condo?"

"I have a letter for you. I'm inside Coop's place. Stop by."

Picking up on Sam's anxiety, Shelly heads home. "Call me if you need to talk. P.S.—I'll help you find a better place!"

The joy from the weekend fades and is replaced with disappointment. Taking slow and deliberate steps, thoughts flood Sam's mind; why didn't Coop call him?

Coop's place looks immaculate. It's usually clean, but cluttered. "Sam, I'm sorry. Coop is being a little paranoid. But then again, I have no idea what's going on. He left the country and I have no idea where he is. He was afraid your phone was hacked so he had a letter messengered to me. He gave me direct orders to burn it after you read it. This is all a little fucked up."

Taking a deep breath, Sam takes the letter and rips it open. A check for $2600 falls on the floor. The memo reads "Security Deposit," but he never gave one.

Dear Sammy,

Sorry for this craziness. I'm sure this is just me being overly neurotic, but this is me trying to protect you, Shelly, and Nina. I want you to find a nice, new place. I gave you a check for your security deposit and first month's. You should try and find something fast. If Shelly is cool, stay at her place until you find something. I'm not sure it's safe here anymore and I have no idea when I'll be back. Wherever you go, I will find you. Only from the library, email me at this address, waltermichael-roenick@gmail. I know Toews is better, but this is my email account. You need to start an email address as well. I'll write when I can. Love you like a brother.

Trying to suck in the tears, Sam hands the note to Nina, who promptly burns it in the sink. Placing his hands over his eyes, as if he just found out a relative died, Sammy breaks down. Nina wraps her arms around Sam and gives him a needed squeeze.

Looking in Coop's fridge, Sam grabs a beer. "What do you know, Nina?"

"I'm not an emotional girl, but I'm sad. Coop made me get my real estate license to help him invest in real estate. He paid for the course, so I figured why not. Now I'm selling his place. I'm the executor of his estate, and he disbanded his company. All in a few days. It's fucking crazy. He was, like, my Yoda."

TRAVEL PLANS

Tossing everything that won't make it through security in a UPS box, Coop stares at Natalie in awe. Even while worried for his life, hers, and his dad's, he can't stop staring at her. "Okay, before I rip off your clothes—what happened with Sal?" While listening, Coop mails out his box to his father's hotel.

The first smile she's had since Coop rescued her is an ear-to-ear grin. "How can you think about sex at a time like this? Men. I needed money so I headed to the boats. Sal's guys noticed me winning and I 'won' a trip to the boss, along with champagne and Belgian chocolates. He said I could gamble more if I made him some money. That was it. I made him a few bucks and he let me go. Said any time I wanted to help again, say the word. It was surprisingly, a nice experience. I was a little shocked."

Sensing she's telling the truth, "You sure we don't have time for a quickie? Why don't you stay here? It's gorgeous. Steve can look out for you, and I'll be back."

Natalie's smile dissipates. "They want me, Coop. They will stop at nothing to get me. I know it's not going to be like it was with Sal, but if I can get them on track financially, maybe I live. If we run, they will find us, and then it will be too late. This is not a Rambo or John McClain situation."

With the *Die Hard* reference, Natalie becomes even hotter to Coop. "Okay. We go together. You give me three days to find Kastric. After that, we are a team. My dad's already there."

Coop's mind is racing. How can he save his father and Natalie? His father has already skipped a few days of taking out money or charging anything. What if they both die? Pushing his mind to be positive, "Let's take a day to do some planning and then fly out."

"Your dad is there; we go now. I'll do some researching online; you be a foot soldier. Let's head there now."

Coop cannot disagree with her plan. The ride to the airport is a geography/smart phone test. Coop answers first, "We can take a flight to anywhere in Europe and then fly to Albania. Turkey is close. Not sure there are a lot of flights from Australia to Turkey."

Natalie figures out the first flight. "Eithad. They fly direct. Next flight is an hour or tomorrow morning." Using a prepaid debit card, "We are on a flight tomorrow morning. Maybe it doesn't have to be a quickie."

HOLES

Getting two bullet holes stitched up in a hotel room feels normal to Fred. He has no idea if the woman sewing him up is a doctor, nurse, or seamstress. Her work is impeccable; the stitches are tight and symmetrical. "You might be the best needle worker I've seen. You fix my shirt, too?"

With a thick accent, "You are lucky these are just surface wounds. Bullet went all the way through your right tricep and the one on your thigh grazed it. Your head, though, is not good. Definitely a concussion. I have no idea the severity. One to ten, what's pain? Ten is the worst."

Thinking about it for a minute, "It was like a six before the drugs. What did you give me?"

As Fred passes out, he hears the woman say, "Wake him every few hours. He'll live."

Ari and Tal try to piece together Fred's limo story. Something does not make sense. Why would he snap? What's his secret? In the meantime, thanks to their smart bullets hitting Kastric's getaway car, they have a location.

Ari takes the first shift and wakes Fred around 10. "Wake up, old man." Bloodshot eyes greet Ari—half opened, of course.

"Fuck. Where are we?" Fred's eyes scan the room. He has no idea how he got wherever they are. "What happened to the hot doctor?"

Almost like a parent would say, "You're okay. We are at a corporate condo near the city. After your hot doctor finished tending to the bullet holes in your arm and leg, she left. We need to get you an MRI tomorrow. You hit the ground and we saw your head bounce up. You remember anything?"

Feeling comfortable with his new friend, "He said something about killing the guy protecting the girl. The girl screwed him out of millions of dollars, just like that guy told us. He thinks she's some genius who can help him make up that loss." Remembering Ari is also in the 5%, "My son is the protector."

Ari takes a deep breath, "So you risked your life to save your son? I get it. Rest up. We got to wake you every few hours."

"I'm fine. I've taken harder hits than that." Before another thought enters his drugged mind, Fred is asleep again.

A phone rings inside Fred's pocket. Ari picks up the phone and tries to sound American. "Howdy."

"Fred, what the hell happened? We found some of your blood on the fucking street. Are you alive? We have video of two men tossing you in a dark van. No plates of course."

Recognizing Tommy's voice, Ari responds, "He's out cold and safe. How the fuck did you let this guy out of your site? He's nuts. I'm assuming you can track the location. Come by and take him to a hospital in another country. His head is swollen like a bowling ball. We got the bullet holes patched. We can talk when you get here."

Tommy is relieved upon hearing Ari's voice. "Man, you guys really are the best. I know you trust no one, but this is a secure line." Ari hangs up before Tommy can ask for more details. Always best to talk in person. His only thought is that they need to jump on Kastric fast. He's going to go into hiding with all the action tonight.

HOTEL MOTEL HOLIDAY INN

As usual, a drink helps calm Coop down. The fresh air and ocean view also help. Natalie seems calm. Her plan is to give herself up. These guys are relentless, and at the end of the day, Kastric wants money more than her dead. Staring at Coop, she relaxes; no one has ever saved her before. The usual guy attracted to her wants arm candy or just sex. Coop wants the whole thing. He's currently daydreaming about rocking in a porch swing with Natalie; this is rare for him.

Feeling her curiosity, Coop opens up. "Girls I date, friends, they all think I have a drinking problem. No one knows it's the only thing that slows down my mind. Weed helps, too, but it leaves a fog the next day. A few drinks dull the visions. I tried meditation, but then I see the future."

Natalie slowly chews a bite of fish that was probably caught a few hours ago. "The feelings come and go for me. When I'm alone, everything is quiet. Meditation, quiet time works for me. Right now, I'm okay. I know this is crazy, but I really enjoy being with you."

With an unforced smile sneaking out of Coop's lips, Natalie can feel him relaxing. "So this is a date, Coop. How do you play the night?"

Trying not to read her mind, "Dessert. We find some amazing dessert."

With a huge grin, "This girl loves dessert. Keep going."

Pointing to the moon, "This place does the hard part for you. I mean, I could never set the mood like those stars bouncing off the water."

The waiter, eavesdropping, brings a cookie skillet with ice cream to their table, and then jokes, "Or I could bring it back to the kitchen."

Natalie strongly responds, "Over your dead body. You might have to bring one for him."

Coop takes the obligatory spoonful and watches Natalie quickly polish off the entire cookie. Interrupting her indulgence, "We could order another one."

With chocolate on her lips, Natalie leans forward and kisses Coop. Leaning into his ear, she whispers, "Can we just have sex right now?"

Overacting, Coop yells, "CHECK! I NEED THE CHECK!"

The rush of joy, the endorphins, is something Coop hasn't felt in a long time. The closest memory is the Olympic trials for judo. Coop had one more match, and if he had won, he would have made the U.S. team. It didn't guarantee him anything, but it was a start. His mom, of course, told him he could never be in the spotlight like that. Coop had no idea he was remotely good enough to get so far. He had been training in martial arts forever, but so had all the other kids. There had to be other 5% athletes in the room. The difference between Coop and the others was that his reflexes were just faster. It's why he was so good at baseball and boxing.

When the bell rang to start the match, Coop attacked first. He tossed this man so fast the ref had to do a double take. Right then, Coop knew he could make the team. That's all he needed. The next match, he let this stocky, smelly kid toss him around like a rag doll. Sammy was watching the fight and came up to him afterwards. "Why are you smiling?"

Tonight trumps losing on purpose. Carrying a slightly drunk Natalie in the sand, Coop kisses her soft, big lips. He melts into them. Warmth covers his body as Natalie pulls him in closer. She whispers again in his ear, and goose bumps form on his neck. "Put me down. Right here."

Like teenagers, they look for a secluded spot to continue; they only take giggling breaks. Natalie pulls a beach towel out from her bag. Coop comments, "Presumptuous?"

Hopping on top of Coop, "We are in Australia. I think it's normal to have a towel." Pulling off her lace underwear, Coop quickly scans for peeping toms. His thoughts are interrupted as Natalie unzips his pants.

Having sex with emotions has been a void for both of them. This feeling of lust before complete uncertainty is a much-needed, delightful respite. Riding Coop is the best sex of Natalie's life. She doesn't care about being loud, that one breast is bigger than another, that she's too skinny, that all the sun has brought out a few freckles—and even if Coop finishes too soon, it'll be amazing.

POSTCARD

Sam has settled into Shelly's place. He signed a lease for next month but part of him and all of Shelly does not want him to go. Unlike women he's dated in the past, Shelly is not crazy. Well, he's learned she's a neat freak but other than that, the only thing they fight about is television and restaurants. Shelly eats Mexican or sushi for most meals, and Sam fears mercury poisoning and taco boredom. And who doesn't love Italian food?

Life without Coop is hard. Sam has other friends but no one who knows him like Coop. And no one can cook like Coop. Turning to Shelly, "I miss the witty banter, and I really miss Coop's cooking."

Opening the mail, Shelly responds, "Maybe this guy, Lucky, can take Coop's place. He or maybe she sent you a postcard."

Lucky was one of the many nicknames Coop had. In college, the good grades, winning poker hands, and sports skills were attributed to Coop's luck. Now Sam knows the truth. His excitement is obvious as he runs into the front room to check out the letter.

Turning to the text side: Miss you a lot, dude. I know the housing situation was a little shocking. Sorry about that. Hope all is well with the girl. I know you hate when I say it, but I knew it would be good. All is well with me. Traveling around the world a bit, feeling like a character on tv. I'm enjoying it more than I thought but man, do I miss egg sandwiches and coffee with you. Have a shot of tequila with a lime for me. Email me. LULAB, Lucky

Judging by Sam's reaction, "How's Coop?"

"You are so smart, babe. My guess, he's not doing so well. I feel bad; he has this desire to save everyone. First me, for stealing his final four picks, now Natalie, and probably his old man. He's been there for me since I was eighteen. I helped him with a computer course, but other than that, he pulled me through classes, we won a bunch of intramural sports because of him, and of course I owe him for introducing us."

Shelly can tell Sam needs to reminisce. He's been a little sad lately and she thought it was because he didn't like living with her. Although she feels bad for her love, she's relieved. "What's your craziest Coop story?"

Shaking his head, "There are just so many. I'm not sure I can nail it down to one." A movie reel plays in Sam's head. Sitting in a soft chair, feeling the fringe of the blanket, it brings him back to camping. "If you said Las, Coop would book the trip before you said Vegas or Angeles. I said I'd never gone camping, and Coop stood up at the top of the bar and yelled out, 'Who wants to pop Sam's camping cherry?'" Coop's dad used to take him camping before he left. Then his mom filled the void. She read books, watched videos, and even took a class. Coop and his mom would take this ridiculously big book around their backyard and see if the plants, bugs, and berries were edible. Coop oddly bragged about his foraging skills."

Sammy's entire demeanor changes. He smiles and continues, "Now, Coop's camping prowess was infamous with photos. He had the giant fish picture, the roaring fire, and there was even a picture of him cooking what looked like a snake over an open fire. I never thought anyone would join us. But a few hands went up. I forgot beer courage. Coop forced our sober friend Ron to drive us in his truck to get supplies. While Coop packed sleeping bags, tents, and blankets, the rest of us drank more and danced to the soundtrack of *Grease*. By the time Coop packed his truck, the group of eight was down to three of us. Coop, this girl Jenny, and I headed to a nearby forest preserve. "

Playing the rest of the night in his head, "It was a fun time. The three of us woke up on a blanket like this frilly one. It was freezing cold; we were in the middle of nowhere. We were in a three-way spoon. We spent the morning eating canned beans and spent the rest of the day nauseous and extremely gassy. After Jenny puked, we decided it was time to go back to campus. Sorry to bore you, Shelly. Just needed to tell a Coop story."

Shelly could see the loneliness in Sam's eyes. Poor guy misses his friend and there's really nothing to do but listen to bad stories but good memories. "Maybe now is time for you to really focus on being a kick-ass marketer, or the best boyfriend ever, or find a way to help Coop."

Sam looks sad and concerned. "I wish I could help him, but how?"

PLAN

Waking up with Natalie in his arms feels normal. Almost like they're an old married couple that still really like each other. Natalie's warm body and smooth, sun-kissed skin begin to get Coop riled up. For Natalive, waking up cuddling with someone she actually cares about is exhilarating. She feels Coop poking her, and not with his hand.

Natalie, more aggressive than Coop, "Let's brush first."

Concern trumps sex, "What are we going to do? My dad is probably dead or close to it, they want you, and they are probably on to me."

Natalie, without pause, "First off, I hope your dad is alive. We'll find him first. Then, I turn myself in. Last night was great. This connection we have is incredible. But you know this guy is not going to stop until he has me. He needs me to make him money. As I start to do that, you try to rescue me. I'm not sure either of us lives that way. It's been a while since my research down there, but I remember his tax bill was ridiculous. The government knows he's shady, so he pays them to keep away."

Coop, staring deeply into her dark eyes, "I'll save you."

When Coop's mom died, he could sense it. He knew the moment she passed away without even trying to think about it.

It started with a visual of the hospital room just popping into his head and then moments later the call came through. With Fred, he sees nothing but a room.

Fred sees nothing but a television. His new friends, Ari and Tal, have been hosting Fred as his injuries heal. They have tracked Kastric's location and are working with the CIA for more intel. While watching *Seinfeld* reruns, Fred checks his bank account. Like clockwork, Coop has been taking out money.

"You sure you want to go back to your hotel, Fred?"

With his usual sarcastic tone, "I love you both and would like to spend more time with my new crew, but it's time for me to be self-sufficient again. I'll miss the hummus."

Ari responds while Tal shakes his head, "Old man, we just bought the hummus from the store. Take it easy. We'll update you when we get some info. We have this stealth droid deployed. We'll get a bunch of pics and sit back with you and your team to discuss next steps. Kastric is going to disappear if we don't jump on it."

Fred senses that Coop is on the way. Since he's been slacking with using the debit card, Fred at least wants to be in the room when Coop comes. As the swelling in his brain fades, Fred's anger grows. If only he could've gotten off a clean shot. Then again, who knows if that was really Kastric.

Walking into his hotel room, Fred lets out a large yawn. Before taking a nap, he scans the room for bugs and cameras. It looks like no one has been in here, but better to be safe than sorry. Aside from the Israelis and his son, no one knows where he's staying. His CIA buddies think he's at their corporate condo but Fred definitely does not trust them.

After a quick scan of the room, Fred draws a picture of Kastric. He does this every time he lies down and when he wakes up, hoping it jogs his memory.

THE GROWING TEAM

Pulling up to the Grand Hotel, Coop's senses are on overdrive. He knows his dad is in room 333. Natalie is impressed. "How do you know the room number?"

"Popped in my head when we walked in. He told me he would register under Greg Brady. I would rather not be seen on that camera. We need to keep our hats and sunglasses on."

After years of wishing his father was dead, it's now the opposite. All the hate, all the missed games, and all the loneliness when his mom died are paused. Coop speed walks to his dad's room. Before reaching the room, Coop turns to Natalie, "He's hurt."

Trying not to knock too hard, Coop can feel his heartbeat through his shirt. Is he too late? Something is not right. The door opens slowly while Coop impatiently knocks. The room is empty, except for some blood on the sheets. Scanning the room, "FRED! FRED! FRED!"

With a huge smile and no shirt on, Fred walks in from the hallway with a bucket of ice. Aside from an egg-shaped bump on his forehead and stitches, Fred looks okay. Embracing Coop with a smile, "I'm okay, Mini."

Emotions rush over Coop. He hasn't been called Mini since he was 7. He looked just like his dad as a child and had the same mind. Both his parents called him Mini, but a few months after his dad left, his mom stopped calling him that. Trying to block out the emptiness, "Old man, your head is bad. You are concussed. I think you are bleeding because the stitches are too tight."

Shaking Natalie's hand, "Nice to meet you dear. Coop, I'm fine. The last scan I had showed the swelling is gone. Rip out these fucking stitches. She did too good of a job. Whoever she was."

"I'll do it in the car. We have to get out of here." Peering out the window, Coop sees an unmarked black sedan idling, and watches two men in suits pop out. "Are those your CIA buddies?"

Fred throws on a shirt and tucks a gun in his pants. He hands another one to Coop and leads them to the cargo elevator. Natalie takes loud breaths to calm down. Her heart rate is skyrocketing, and her olive skin is pale. They run out of the elevator a floor early and head for the stairs. Coop lets out a fake smile. "Just another day with the Coopers."

Turning to his dad, "They have a guy outside each exit. They probably spotted Natalie at the airport. I was wearing a hat and sunglasses. Give me your shirt, old man." Coop swaps shirts with Fred and kicks the door open, but doesn't step out. The hesitation leads to confusion.

Kastric's goon pops his head inside. Coop punches him in the nose and then pulls him inside by the ears. A quick blow to the back of the head and the guy passes out. Fred hands the unconscious man's gun to Natalie.

"This one is simple—aim with both hands and squeeze the trigger." Natalie nods her head yes. The back of the hotel is quiet. Fred is whispering into his phone as they walk towards the street. "We've been spotted and are trying to get away. Where's your car?"

Even though the volume is low, Coop can tell he's not talking to Americans. Within seconds, a dark van cuts into the back alley of the hotel. Fred's new friends might have saved the day. Before Kastric's men make it to the other side, Coop and his new team escape capture.

Ari comments first, "Our team is growing. Glad we stuck around the hotel."

"Thanks for saving us. You got water for her?"

Handing her an IDF water canteen, Ari introduces himself. "I'm Ari, Tal is driving. I can tell you the plan from the CIA is to give you up. Kastric is a powerful man. The images we have from his fort are intense. I'm not sure how we break in. Ever since Fred almost killed him, Kastric has been MIA. Their government is afraid of Kastric. Your secret agents are, too."

Coop's mind races for a plan. "You guys and I dress up like members of the lawn crew. We get inside, figure out where he is, kill him, drive right out."

Natalie looks at Coop like he's crazy. Nothing is that easy. Ari, with excitement in his tone, "You are onto something. There's a crew in one of our drone pictures. With a space that big, they must do work constantly."

A quick search on his phone and Ari finds the landscaping company. Tal yells out, "We got trouble!"

Two black Range Rovers are on each side of their van. Natalie, with her heart racing, "I'm giving myself up. You guys come and rescue me."

A window of one of the Rovers comes down. "Hand over the girl. We got an exchange for you. She will not get hurt. Kastric wants to make his money back. Once she does that, she's free to go."

A thin man with round glasses and duct tape over his mouth is kicked out of the other Range Rover. Ari turns to Tal. "IT'S OREN!"

Natalie and Coop hold each other tightly. "I'll find you!" With a short kiss, Natalie bravely walks out of the van holding back tears,and all the fear.

As Natalie walks away, Ari puts a hand on Coop's back. "We'll save her, my friend. And Oren will help us. We've been waiting for him. He's one of our guys. A scientist."

Oren pops in the van and exchanges hugs with Tal and Ari. Ari rips off the duct tape and after a short wince, Oren is back to smiling. "I told you I would be okay! Good to see you boys. Who are you two?"

"This is Coop and Fred. Long story short, that's his girl. We need to get her back. Now fill us in."

Oren guzzles the water bottle next to him and wipes sweat off his thick brow. "She'll be fine. They want to test her. Taking blood, DNA, scans. They are about five years behind us. They just tested me and discussed my studies."

All eyes are laser focused on Oren. Coop might be looking at him and even listening, but he's only thinking about Natalie. With every inch of his mind, Coop tries to read the future. All he sees is that Natalie is alive.

Oren continues to describe the facility. The moment they reach the hotel, Oren draws the facility. From the testing rooms to the main gate, no detail is left out. Coop realizes his skill is memory. It's like watching an architect draw a home.

MOVING PAINS

Shelly's place is now completely cramped with Sam's stuff and her clothes. While Sam builds some extra shelves, Shelly walks into the guest room, which is filled with Sam's exercise equipment. Rifling through the boxes, Shelly has no idea what half these things are for. "Sam, come here."

She holds up a pair of sticks. "What is all of this stuff?"

"Filipino fighting sticks, grappling dummy, Thai boxing pads, boxing bag. And those are exercise bands."

With a confused look, Shelly asks, "Who are you?"

Sam smiles. "Coop gave me most of this stuff. We trained together. His baseball coach made him quit the judo club and boxing. He had this amazing sophomore year, and everyone thought he was going pro. "

Shelly, still looking confused, "What does that have to do with you, and why was he so obsessed with fighting?"

"I always wanted to learn martial arts, so when he couldn't train around school, he started training me. His parents got him hooked. His dad wanted him to be a boxer; his mom pushed judo."

Shelly grabs the fighting sticks. "Can you show me?"

With no hesitation, "Of course. Coop and I have been training together for years. I picked up a few things."

Looking at all the equipment, Sam feels nostalgic. How did he never realize Coop was in the 5%? The guy was a great athlete, on the honor roll, a ladies' man, and never worked that hard except during their workouts. Twice a week they would punch, kick, and flip each other until they were ready to pass out. He only saw Coop get in one fight, which he quickly won. From joint locks to pressure points, Sam received a PhD in martial arts.

Turning to Shelly, "I never thought it was odd that Coop knew all this stuff. I just thought he wanted to be an MMA fighter. He did try out for the U.S. judo team." Pulling out a rubber gun, "It's crazy, he even taught me gun defense."

Intrigued, Shelly asks, "What happened?"

With a smile, "Coop was awesome. He was tossing guys around, match after match. I thought for sure he was going to make it. In the semifinal round he tossed his opponent to the ground in, like, two seconds. It was amazing. The next match was longer, and the guy somehow beat Coop. Now I get it—Coop probably threw the match."

Puzzled, Shelly asks the obvious question: "Why?"

Smiling, Sam finally gets it, "I didn't know it then, but he probably thought they would figure out he was in the five percent. He smiled like he won, and I thought it was weird. Now I get it—he knew he could've won."

THE COMPOUND

Huge gates open at a snail's pace. Natalie's heart is pounding through her shirt. Taking deep breaths, she tries to control her emotions. Looking at the men in the car, all she senses is confusion—as if they are thinking, "Why this woman? She doesn't look special."

Interrupting her thoughts and the silence, "You are here for science and retribution. Do not fear death."

The gates slam shut moments after opening. The compound is a huge brick mansion. Random trucks, cars, and two limos line the driveway. Walking in, Natalie holds back her tears. She focuses on cleanliness. Did they vacuum, dust, and disinfect just for her? The compound is impeccably clean.

A short bald man greets Natalie as she enters. He hands her slippers, and, in a thick Eastern European accent, says, "Your shoes, please."

Slowly taking off her neon running shoes, Natalie asks, "That's how you keep it so clean in here?"

"Cleanliness is important to the boss. He left instructions for you. He's out of town indefinitely. Cooperate and you will be out of here in a few days. We will send for clothes, or you borrow."

Without thinking, "How long is he detained for?"

With a big smile, "You are good. He was right about you. Very good. I'm Gunther. We have tests for you and want financial tips. Kastric was very impressed by you. Coffee, tea, or water?"

Pointing at the coffee mug, Gunther follows through with a cup of coffee. He pours himself tea, and places both mugs on the large kitchen table. "Tell me your skill?"

Natalie's mind wanders; she thinks Kastric is stuck in the U.S. How is he able to run things if he's behind bars? Maybe he's working with someone else? Must be working with Sal. Most inmates can't find a job when they get out, and Sal's running a corporation from inside.

The caffeine helps Natalie refocus. "I sense emotions. From those, I draw conclusions. They're not always right, but most of the time I'm close. I can't pick winning lotto numbers or see the future. Working in finance, I was able to read into a company and sense if they were moving in the right direction and ethical. If you let me look at your portfolio, I can make suggestions. What's your skill?"

"I know when people lie. Follow me."

Gunther leads Natalie into some sort of game room. A few chess tables sit out, a ping pong table is slightly out of place in the middle of the room, books line several shelves, and video games are stacked next to a flatscreen. "Natalie, you learn a lot about the gifted in this room. The quick thinkers are amazing at video games and ping-pong; someone like you, cards or chess."

Natalie has not played chess in years. She was her high school's best chess player and, according to her father, did not practice enough to become a national champ. The truth was, she got bored of wasting most of her weekends at competitions. "Gunther, if you want a game, all you have to do is ask."

Without being asked, "My job is to evaluate you. There will be a nurse in the morning who will take some blood, run images, and swab your cheek. You have nothing to worry about. Kastric is a scientist and a socialist."

"You mean capitalist."

Gunther smiles, "Ah, a funny girl. I like it. Quick wit is another intelligence marker."

RESCUE

Pacing around the small hotel room, Coop tries to hatch a plan. Oren interrupts his thoughts. "Coop, she will be fine. Give it a few days. I'm surprised they did not take you, too."

The room grows quiet, and everyone looks at Oren. "I mean, they didn't know how all their men kept disappearing, trying to capture a young lady. These are military men, like U.S. Special Forces."

Fred smiles with pride. Ari chimes in, "Okay, well, special agent Coop needs to calm the fuck down."

With a deep inhale and long exhale, Coop asks, "Oren, they read your mind in there?"

Nodding yes, "Probably. These men want money and weapons. They want to develop an army of five percent and sell DNA. It's like a Matt Damon film, but they are building the brain first; then Kastric sells it to the highest bidder. Natalie is there because they think her stock advice is valuable. They think she can predict outcomes. Not sure if that's her skill."

Fred chimes in, "We can't just sit here and hope they don't kill her." As his brain heals, his mind is starting to work again. The current movie in his head is action packed: bombs going off around the compound, night vision goggles, sniper on a power line, and a few more guys running in to save Natalie.

Coop turns to Oren, "Can they create a super team?"

Oren laughs, "Don't you think we would have that? Too many variables. Being in the five percent is not always hereditary. Also, the skill set is so different. You could probably build one hell of a chess team, but that might even be nurture over nature. What they should be studying are brain hacks like coffee, nicotine, word searches, puzzles, supplementation, sleep. You see, everyone has the same brain more or less, it's just that the connections are different."

Fred interjects, "So you guys are using brain hacks to improve your skills?"

Oren answers for team Israel. "Yes. Nothing too sophisticated, but we have workshops and mess around with light, games, memory tests, that stuff."

All eyes fall on Oren. "Google it later. Fred, get your FBI/CIA buddies on the horn. Maybe we can track down Kastric."

The room falls silent as Fred tracks down his U.S. contacts. The energy in the room is low; Oren is falling asleep on the couch and Coop's amazed that no one is as concerned as he is. He's only known Natalie for a few weeks, but he's never had this connection with anyone.

Like a bolt of electricity, it hits Coop. "This is a ruse. Kastric is in the States."

Fred stops dialing and starts thinking: Building a 5% army in the U.S. with the mob boss behind bars. "Holy shit. I'm so dumb." The rest of the room looks confused as Coop starts packing up his clothes.

Ari loudly asks, "What gives?"

Coop explains that with the mob boss in jail, it's prime time for Kastric to hunt down 5% members in the U.S. "Being in jail, Sal's still working and Kastric has a lot of money. He's also connected. He's going to get his hands on a list, and one by one, bribe, kidnap or just pay guys to join his army."

Coop's worry bounces back and forth from Sam to Natalie. Sam is one hell of a fighter, but can he take a guy that sees what's going to happen, before it happens? And Natalie, on the other hand, could still be in serious trouble, but his gut says she'll be fine. They want her to make some investing suggestions and run through a litany of tests. She might not need rescuing.

Fred can see the conflict in his son. "Stay here with my IDF buddies. Once Natalie is released, come to the States. Besides, I have connections on all sides. I'll find that asshole, and this time I won't let him get away."

The trouble with Coop is that he doesn't trust the old man either. Sure, he's been sober the past few weeks, but what's his angle?

"Fred, let me have the secure phone." With a cryptic text, he reaches out to Sam. "Keep UR eyes open. Good time for a vacay. LULAB." When Coop graduated, he used to end his calls with Sam, "Love you like a brother." Hopefully, Sam figures it out.

Next step is to text Mr. Good Life. "MGL! Sell IGE. One last favor. Take my buddy on a boat trip. Respond with emoji." After a few seconds of waiting, a thumbs-up emoji comes through. Coop breathes a sigh of relief. That should buy him a few more days here before Kastric tracks down Sam. Who knows? Sam might not even be on the list. As his mom used to say, "A little caution goes a long way."

Fred takes the phone back and dials up his boss. A short conversation ends with, "I'll see you when I land."

The Israelis head to their room, allowing a little father–son time. Coop is sure they sense the dysfunctional relationship that has been improving steadily. Coop never thought he would be sad to see his dad go, but he is. After all these years, the childhood memories have been playing on repeat since the day Fred stumbled back into his life.

Fred never cared if Coop was the best at anything but pushed him physically the way his mom pushed him mentally. Between sports and all the exercise equipment a boy could dream of, it was a constant training session. It's like they both prepared him for this life. If you can call it that.

A tight hug by Fred melts away a little resentment. Fighting a tear, Fred says, "I know sorry means nothing. But I'm sorry. I was such a screw up. You've got to understand I was trying to save you. I was wrong. What I had to do was sober up, get a normal job, and raise you. I never stopped thinking of you and loving you."

Pulling out Coop's college baseball card, Fred says, "Memories of our epic battles and this card have always been with me. Sign it."

The emotional turmoil is new to Coop, too. The closest relationships he's had, aside from his mom, have been Sam and, recently, Natalie. He just didn't allow people to get to know him. He signs the card 'Coop' and adds a heart. "Get out of here. Don't get killed. You still owe me like a thousand ice cream cones and trips to the arcade. Save my friend."

Watching his dad walk out of the room brings back old memories. He used to get so angry with his mom because she couldn't shoot a basket to save her life. At six years old he could beat her at one-on-one. He missed the competition that his dad brought. Fred wouldn't let him win at anything. "One day you'll beat me at everything. It will just happen. And the weird thing is that part of you will be sad."

Boxing was the best with his dad. Fred would wrap Coop's hands real tight, put gloves on him, and they would spend hours throwing punches, blocking, and hitting the heavy bag. Eventually Coop tore up the heavy bag with a bat.

"I was so mad at you after you left. I took a bat and destroyed the heavy bag. Tears streamed down my face, and Mom said nothing. She just hugged me. That day, that cold winter day, I decided I wouldn't need you anymore. I was seven."

Tears burn as they form in Fred's usually dry eyes. Focusing on his backpack instead of facing his son, guilt overtakes him. A few deep breaths help to calm him down. A little shocked that worked. With remorse, "I know, buddy. I missed you. Every day. It was hard. I was just such a fuckup. I mean, I drank every night until I passed out on the couch. The best part was in the morning. You would walk down the steps super quiet, jump on me, and give me the best morning hugs. That was the highlight of my life." Pulling out an old picture of the two of them on the couch, Fred adds, "You were a great kid. I didn't want you to be a loser like me. Emma was perfect. Smart, sweet, loving. I knew you would be better off without me. Trust me, I saw the movie play over and over. If I stayed, we all died young."

Coop relaxes his shoulders and lies on the bed, gazing out the window. "Mom was the best."

As Fred walks out the door, "Agreed. I love you. See you in the States."

WAITING GAME

The mental tests don't fatigue Natalie. Mental endurance she has, physical endurance, not so much. Isaac, her proctor for the day, is worn out. "You are doing very well. Let's call it a day. Tomorrow you go home."

The few days of testing, blood samples, saliva and rest have been way less invasive than Natalie thought. She's only spoken to Gunther and Isaac. Trying to get Isaac to talk, Natalie starts asking questions. She can tell he likes to talk. "The past few days I've been poked, prodded and quizzed. I even gave you stock tips and analysis. How did I compare to others?"

Trying to look coy, "You did well. Smart girl. You are not one that really sees the future, but you have lots of strengths." Pulling out a list, Isaac rattles off basic info. "Comprehension is off the charts. You retain information very well. Equations solid, emotional IQ incredible, and I have no idea about DNA. Those results I'm not privy to."

As Isaac continues his analysis, it hits Natalie, "I've never been used as a decoy before."

With a smile, "You read situations well. Kastric wanted you here for several reasons. None of us know his real plan. We are hired help. That's all, not even in his army. The guards are a different story."

Before the two can continue to talk, a guard comes by with her phone. "Call your friends. Tell them tomorrow at ten a.m. we drop you off."

Jumping out of bed, Coop picks up the phone as fast as his fingers will allow. "Hello? Did they hurt you? Are you okay?"

With the guard using his fingers to indicate hurry, Natale tries to talk but words don't come out. A tear sneaks down her face and the guard feels slightly bad. He holds up two fingers and offers her a little space.

"I'm fine. Really. Some tests, nothing too bad. Tomorrow at ten in the morning they will drop me off at the hotel."

"You have no idea how excited we will be to see you. All of us." Coop figures they are listening to the call. He wants them to think they have numbers, that there's an army waiting for her.

As the guard takes Natalie's phone, he adds, "Go to the library. You can read or watch some television."

Natalie's short list of boyfriends could be counted on one hand. Whatever this experience with Coop is, it's by far the most emotional. Then again, it's hard not to be emotional when you think someone's trying to kill you. Over the phone, she can sense the love in Coop's voice.

VACATION

Shelly, holding Sam's phone, "What does LULAB mean? Someone sent you a very cryptic text."

Without hesitation, "Love you like a brother. It's Coop." Grabbing the phone, Sam's heart rate shoots through the roof. Something is going on.

Shelly, new to this type of stressful situation, starts packing. Watching his girlfriend speed pack like she's a contestant on *The Amazing Race*, Sam asks, "Where are you going?"

Passionately kissing Sam, "We are a team, baby. We are getting out of Dodge! I'm up for a vacation." His admiration for Shelly continues to grow and amaze him. After thanking Coop in his mind for bringing them together, Sam starts packing, too.

Searching flights on her phone, Shelly realizes flying on a Friday night is not cheap. "What if we drive somewhere?" Sam's phone rings and Shelly yells out, "COOP?"

"Close. It's Mr. Good Life." Focusing on the phone call, all Shelly can ascertain is they are going on a boat.

Mr. Good Life has invited them to sail around Lake Michigan for the weekend—maybe longer, depending on work. His boat has two rooms, two bathrooms, but only one shower. Good thing no one gets seasick.

Heading to the street, Sam gets paranoid. People everywhere are walking around, but one man is staring a little too hard. The second the random stranger turns his head, Sam grabs his girlfriend's hand and quickly hops in a cab. "Sorry. There was some weird guy looking at us." Now turning to the cab, "To Belmont Harbor, please. Just head east."

When the cab stops, they speedwalk away. Heading toward the marina, Sam senses someone is following them. Whispering in Shelly's ear, "You walk towards the playground. I'll text you to head to the boat when the coast is clear." With a hug and kiss, Shelly walks away, confused, with all the luggage. Sam sits down on the closest bench and casually looks around. No sign of the stranger. Well, except for the guy that just sat down. Sam takes a deep breath and grabs the man's crotch, tightly.

Wincing, "FBI. Please let go of my junk. Badge is in front vest pocket. Fred sent me to check on you."

Reaching into his pocket, Sam looks at his badge and lets go. "Make this quick."

"Be careful, Sam. Trust no one. We have no idea what's going on. Fred has us all on high alert looking for a threat that was just spotted in NYC. My name is Colt; call me if you see anything." Colt walks away just as his contact info appears in Sam's phone.

Quickly catching up to Shelly, the couple head together down to the marina. Shelly's mouth drops. Sam, confused and now amazed, reacts to seeing his vacation boat, "Holy shit. MGL, that's like over fifty feet!"

With the usual smile, "Sixty-two, but who's counting? I share it with a few other guys. I've been lucky, real lucky. And the only way to enjoy it is with friends. Glad you two could make it. I'm telling you, there is nothing like boat fun! Come on in."

The inside of the yacht feels very James Bond. The rectangular couch below deck is white, along with the cabinets in the attached kitchen. The master bedroom has a circular bed, a white-mink rug on the floor, and a flat screen. The other bedroom is smaller, and the couple might argue over who sleeps in the top bunk. Shelly, never afraid to speak up, asks, "Bunk beds? Really, MGL?"

"Hey, those are full-sized bunk beds. You two can easily fit in the top or the bottom one. This was built for partying, anyway—not sleeping."

With that, MGL hands them each a can of cider.

Shelly cocks her head to the side, "Really? Cider?"

Laughing, MGL responds, "Penny loves these, and I'm secure enough in my masculinity to drink them. They taste like candy."

With a sip and a smile, Sam's anxiety level begins to drop.

CHANGE IN PLANS

Fred touches down in the U.S., and his ride to the local FBI office in New York is met with information. Kastric is working with the mob but he's getting greedy. While the boss is locked up, he's purchased lists from him. Kastic wants one of two types of people: young, fit, undereducated men, and scientists. He has a simple test to determine if these people are really in the 5%. With his bank roll, he offers lucrative money for them to join his team.

Relaying the intel to his son, Fred is nervous what Coop will do with it. "I think they are going to take your girlfriend to Italy. I could be wrong. Kastric is investing in a winery, and he has some science geek in Florence. He's diversifying his portfolio and trying to get hedge fund guys and the uber rich to invest. And this might surprise you: The guy you call MGL is on the five percent list. Sam is not."

A stabbing pain behind Coop's eyes blurs his vision. "Shit, I just sent Sam to MGL."

"Don't worry about it. We have eyes on Sam. Are you going to Italy or heading to the States? I also think they are afraid of you. They'll keep her, so you follow."

Coop adds, "I'll head to Italy and send our Israeli friends your way. I'll see you in a few days, hopefully." The phone call ends abruptly as Natalie's number pops up. All Coop can think, that was fast.

With anxiety in her voice, "Change of plans. I'm going on a trip. I'll be back in three days. Four, tops." Before Coop can respond, the line goes dead.

After purchasing his ticket to Florence, Coop heads upstairs to see Tal, Ari, and Oren. The men are all packed up. Oren greets Coop first, "Shalom! I'm heading back to Israel. Want to come? Despite the news, it's safer than this place. I'm going to leave you with the only real info we have on improving your skills. Remember, alcohol dulls the senses, but caffeine and nicotine seem to enhance it. Nothing crazy, but a piece of gum and two cups of coffee worked best in our study."

Ari hands Coop a few packets of nicotine gum. "Don't overdo it or you get a headache. What's your plan?"

"I'm going to Italy to get Natalie back. I'll sneak up on them. I know it's not the best plan. They are trying to keep us apart, and I don't think it's just because they think we're a couple. Then it's off to the USA."

Oren pats Coop on the back. "Check out Florence and Sicily. A world-renowned scientist works between those cities. His name is Lorenzo Acholi. He probably wants fresh stem cells for testing. Look online for his address."

Ari interjects, "Be safe. See you in the States."

While in flight, Coop tries to relax. As of now, no one knows what Coop looks like and that comforts him. Since he found her in Australia quickly, Italy, in theory, should be easier. After finishing his second cup of coffee, Coop starts chewing the nicotine gum. It tastes minty but with a slight off-putting aftertaste. As his knee shakes, he starts visualizing different vineyards. Sicily pops into his brain. With many Vineyards, it's a pretty safe bet.

Once the plane lands in Florence, Coop looks for the first flight to Sicily. The caffeine starts to take a greater effect. Coop's hearing is stronger than it's been before. He can hear Natalie but not see her.

Craning his neck around the airport, Coop can't spot her anywhere. Was her voice just in his head? Taking a few deep breaths,

Coop closes his eyes. His mom used to play this game where they would go to a busy park, and he would have to find his mom. It was hide and go seek meets *Where's Waldo*.

Peaking outside the airport, through the window, Coop sees Natalie getting into a car. Three men are with her, including the driver. They must be sticking around here for a bit.

Hopping in a cab, Coop uses his rusty Italian to give the driver directions. He senses they are headed to a hotel to park their stuff before they sightsee. When they stop, Coop has his driver continue a few seconds longer before getting dropped off on the other side of the street.

With his mind buzzing, he watches as Natalie and two goons step out of the car. He senses Natalie having her own room, but it's a private house, not a hotel. Analyzing a few options, Coop decides to wait for them to move again before attacking. Why would the driver leave the car running if they were going to be a while?

Ducking into a hardware store across from the house, Coop picks up a few essentials: duct tape, zip ties, matches, a mallet, and insect explosives (tear gas). Always with an eye out the window, he catches Natalie's eyes as she heads back to the car.

Sensing a warm feeling, Natalie scans her surroundings. The hat and sunglasses don't fool her. With a quick exchange of smiles, the little red car heads down the street. With all the traffic, Coop keeps up with a fast walk. The nicotine continues to keep his mind a step ahead. Motioning for a cab, he knows exactly where they are going.

It's been a while since Coop has been here, but the shopping district is not far from here. At this time of day, it will be packed with tourists and venders. Maybe they are doing this because they know they're being followed. Coop takes this as a challenge, the situation brings him a hint of joy.

SMOOTH SAILING

The ship is so smooth in the water, Sam doesn't feel the need to take a pill for motion sickness. The beautiful view should calm him down, but it doesn't. MGL, sensing Sam's stress, "Sam, buddy, you're on a boat with a beautiful, beautiful girl by your side. Why are you stressed?"

"I appreciate you taking us on this getaway. This boat is amazing. I'm just worried about Coop. Something is not right."

MGL hands Sam and Shelly a beer and tries to alleviate Sam's concern. "Coop is a machine. His tips have made me a fortune. Dude is a winner. Whatever shit he's in, he'll figure it out. The real question is, what trouble are we in? I hired his old assistant, Nina. It's a little weird because we dated a while back, but she showed me his model for investing—it's amazing. And look at his life: baseball stud, boxer, all around good guy. We need to be more worried about ourselves."

Shelly starts to feel nervous again. "What do you mean?"

"I have no idea. But he brings us together to watch over each other. He's trying to help us. I just don't know what it's from."

Sam starts laughing. "The guy is a genius. He's trying to get us away from chaos. I did something stupid and he's worried either the mob or some other criminal will be coming for me."

MGL comments, "Let's enjoy the next few days. We have plenty of food and, more importantly, lots of wine. I also have a few guns below deck."

Intuitively, Shelly asks MGL, "Are you some sort of spy?"

A little bit of guacamole flies out of MGL's mouth, as he laughs, "I'm a lot of things, Shelly, but spy is not one of them. How about this? When we get back to land, I'll check on Coop. We have lots of mutual acquaintances. I'll make sure he's okay. Promise."

Wrapping her toned arms around Sam, "And I promise to help relax you, completely."

MGL, laughing, "I'm going to just throw out the sheets when we dock."

DEAL OR NO DEAL

The Pentagon is not a place Fred enjoys being in. It's sterile, a maze, and most of his peers have not been in the field for half as long as he has. Specifically, Agent Richardson, a talking head who spent maybe a year outside the office. His speeches are like sermons and the bureaucracy he creates has never helped Fred.

Interrupting Richardson's latest rant, "Agent, take a breath. Your intel is pretty week. With the mob behind bars, Kastric is going to be stealing people. He doesn't care about the gambling or the drug sales. Kastric is building a team of super warriors and super investors. Let me follow Sal's list and we'll catch Kastric. Trust me, Sal's not a fan of Kastric but will take his cash."

The brain trust in the room doesn't want to listen to Fred, but they all know he's right. Luckily, everyone is sick of Richardson talking, which overrides the lack of trust in Fred.

Bob Giles, the highest-ranking official in the room, nods his head yes. "Fred, you have three days. Leverage your relationship with the mob. Agents Murray and Clay will be your help." With a stern stare aimed at Fred, "None of your rogue antics. The political ramifications are something I will not be able to shield you from."

Walking out of the room, Fred's mind replays Giles's comment about politics. Is the U.S. paying Kastric for soldiers? Why would anyone care if Kastric is alive or dead? The mob obviously will take his money, but they don't like him.

Sensing something is up, Fred takes a deep breath and tries to relax his mind. These two agents must know something. It's been a long time since he's tried to read someone's mind, but Agent Clay works in intel and must be hiding something. He's just too quiet.

After a few more breaths, Fred's brain starts to work. A movie plays out: Kastric offering agents to the FBI for money and amnesty. What Fred doesn't know is whether the deal is a ruse to capture a criminal or shady politics.

THE DOCTOR IS IN

Natalie and her guards walk up a three-story office building. A few steps away, Coop watches them buzz office 310. Just before the door closes, Coop steps in. Taking the stairs, Coop beats them up to the third floor but waits, with an ear pressed to the door. His heart is pounding as he listens to Dr. Lorenzo greet everyone.

With a thick accent, but perfect English, "Hello, Natalie. Welcome to my lab. We just want to get a few swabs of your DNA and some stem cells. I promise it won't hurt at all."

As the door closes, Coop peeks into the hallway. One of Kastric's men is standing there silently. Coop waves to the man and mutters, "Buongiorno," and, with an open palm, he slaps the guy in the chin, knocking him out.

After dragging the goon into the hallway, Coop grabs his gun and his phone. Scrolling, he sees Kastric's number. He steals the SIM card and puts his duct tape to work. As the man starts to regain consciousness, Coop knocks him out again. With one last piece of tape over his mouth, Coop heads back to the office.

Quickly organizing a plan, Coop waits patiently for someone to pop out. Hopefully, the other goons come out one at a time looking for this guy. A loud yell, "Freedo! Freedo! Quit messing around! The girl passed out. This might take a while, get in here!"

When no one responds, goon number two pops outside. Coop grabs his arm and locks up his head until the giant goes limp. After smashing his phone, Coop ties him up. As he opens his new hiding spot for bad guys, his first capture, blinded, kicks his friend in the crotch. Goon number two loudly crashes down a few flights of stairs. Coop knows the last goon is sure to follow.

The last guard runs into the hallway and immediately sees his friend. He rips off the tape over his mouth. "Fuck, that hurt. Must be the Chicago guy. Go to bottom of the steps." Without freeing his friend, the last guard runs down the steps. Under the steps, Coop grabs the guys jeans and the stocky man tumbles. A shot rips through the hallway, ricocheting and echoing loudly. Coop, hiding underneath the stairs, seems safe. The noise is sure to garner lots of attention.

Bounding up the steps, Coop is greeted by Lorenzo. "You need to get out of here quickly. With the girl. Kastric is sure to send others. She's fine, just lightheaded."

Tossing her over his shoulder like she's a sack of potatoes, Coop heads in the elevator. When the door opens, his gun is ready for more bad guys. After a quick glance, Coop, heads out the front door. Natalie winks at him as he steps outside. He asks, "Can you run?"

THE SECOND FAVOR

With no judgment—only curiosity—Sam asks, "I figured you would have some deck shoes, but what are those?"

MGL, with an embarrassed smile, "If you couldn't tell, I like my toys. They are light weight and track my running, location, pace, and distance. I have a Garmin, too. Coop forwarded me the link for these. I think he was joking but I bought a pair, and we compare runs."

The sun begins to set and there's nothing but clear blue sky over Lake Michigan. MGL, Sam and Shelly are soaking up the remaining bits of sun and wine. A first, total silence among the three is interrupted by MGL's phone.

A voice he hasn't heard in a long time startles him. "Hello, stranger. What's going on?"

With his burner phone close to his face, Fred softly asks, "I need another favor—can you make it to New York by ten a.m. Friday?"

Trying to play it cool, MGL smiles. "Sure. Hey, you only get one more after this."

Fred responds with a thanks and hangs up. A curious Shelly asks, "That was a short and odd conversation."

"The man on the other line saved my life." Holding hands and their wine glasses, the couple leans in, waiting for details.

"I was young, broke, doing magic on the street in New York. No joke. The minute I got enough cash, I bought cocaine or heroin. Not a proud moment. This guy, like a fairy godfather, looks at me and says, 'I see you living in a condo, plane, boat, Beemer, Chicago.' Oddly, that's where I wanted to move, but drugs owned me. This fortune teller of a guy gets me clean. Lets me stay at his house. It was the strangest and nicest thing. I start day trading with the money he and his friends pay me to clean, grocery shop, and take care of dogs. I kid you not—eight months I lived with this guy. Since he traveled, he wasn't there much so it was a lot of trust. He gave me a few tips on trading, buys me this software and I'm grinding out gains. He drove me back to Chicago. Like a mob boss, he tells me, 'One day I'll ask for a favor.'"

The look of shock is tattooed on both of his guests' faces. Shelly, of course, speaks first, "No fucking way! That's like a movie. You said something like you only get one more after this. What else has he asked you to do?"

With a grin, "Funny you should ask. After telling me nothing about himself, he takes me to a bar in Chicago and says, "Here's my favor. I have a son, means the world to me. Just check on him from time to time." And that was it. Every few months he would stop in Chicago, or we would grab a coffee in NYC."

A little uncertain whether he should tell them Coop is the son, MGL grabs a bottle of water and waits for Shelly to ask another question. He can tell she's trying to put it all together. With a deep gaze, "How do you know Coop again?"

Without lying, "Remember how I hired Nina, my old girlfriend? She was working at the Board of Trade and waiting tables, and hated both jobs. Coop was eating where she worked and noticed her love of the market. He treated Nina exceptionally well. Taught her his method. It was really cool." It was serendipitous how it all worked out. It's also the restaurant where MGL met Nina.

Sam, who's been quiet the entire conversation, finally adds, "I remember the first time we met you. We needed an extra for flag football, and Nina was bragging about your height. Not your skill or the fact you played college ball, but your height."

While Sam and Shelly exchange drunk flirtations, MGL reserves a room in New York and makes sure his plane will be ready to go. It's been a long time since Fred dialed in a favor.

AFTERNOON RUN

The Sicilian sun is beating down on Natalie. She's not in marathon condition like Coop. "I can't keep up, Coop." Realizing a piggyback ride would look odd, Coop waves down a taxi. Coop's mind is a computer; there are four international airports around here. He tells the driver, "Take us to the closest international airport."

As they head towards this tiny airport, Natalie finally starts breathing normally. "Where are we going?"

"How about Morocco? I feel like Kastric has eyes all over Europe. We should be able to catch a flight."

The cab driver, who speaks excellent English, interjects, "You can take a six-hour flight, bus, or even a boat. Flying is the best bet. Go online and buy your tickets quickly, it will be cheaper than at the airport."

With no phone, Natalie watches Coop use his and book two tickets for under $400. Looking up from his phone, Coop plants a kiss on Natalie. The spark is still there. With a caring tone, "What happened to you?"

"It was like they were giving me odd IQ-like tests all day long. I played games. I also suggested a bunch of stocks and that was it. At night, a chef cooked us meals and we read books. It was oddly relaxing. Except today. I sensed you were close. Out of the corner of my eye, I spotted you on the street. The fainting was fake. I was trying to buy you time. When one guard yelled for the other, I knew you were there. Don't you think they'll try the airport?"

Opening his backpack, Coop shows Natalie the wallets and passports he took. "Phones are all busted. No money. Two of them tumbled down the steps. One has a broken leg; the other one is much worse."

Reaching back into his bag, Coop pulls out a hat for Natalie, big sunglasses, a hoodie, and workout pants. With a surprised look, she changes in the cab. "Impressive, guessing my size."

Continuously scanning the window, Coop doesn't sense they are being followed. Channeling his dad, a movie plays in his head. The couple is lying next to each other, on a bed, safe and extremely happy for the moment.

"I hope you can run in those. Our flight boards shortly. Also, on this tiny Island there are several airports. I'm banking they still don't know what I look like, and you look much different. They will assume we fly to Spain, or another big country to catch a flight back to the U.S."

With a smile, Natalie leans in and kisses Coop. She lets out a deep breath, "Then what?"

Shrugging his board shoulders, "We'll have to figure that out."

Exiting the cab, Coop hands the driver a huge wad of cash. "Do me a favor, take the next few days off. You never saw any Americans."

Looking at the pile of cash, "I'm off all week. I'm heading to Paris for a vacation. Thanks, and be safe."

HOOKAH BAR AND TACOS

Although he fakes it well, Fred is constantly paranoid. In his mind, which is not always right, he thinks someone is following him. Glancing at the reflections in windows he passes, he checks for oddities. All hotel rooms are thoroughly inspected for listening devices, and he's always scanning benches and bushes for a spy taking his picture. MGL would know if they were being followed or listened to, but he appeases Fred and meets him at a hookah bar in New York—one with a fireplace, where Fred can burn the handwritten note he hands MGL.

The seedy bar is dark and smells floral. Without a hug or any other greeting, Fred plops down next to MGL, right in front of a giant hookah and next to a fireplace. Taking out a notebook, Fred rips off a page and hands it to Rob.

> *Kastric is a bad man. He's in the States tracking down 5% to sell to the highest bidder. Pure speculation, I think the U.S. is a buyer. They seem hesitant to capture, kill, imprison ... Seems shady. I have two partners that know something but won't talk. I need you to read their minds and fill me in. A few lives are at stake: Coop's, his girlfriend, me and you. Your name popped up on a list. I am meeting agents for an*

*update at this taco place, Chupo's. If you can still read minds,
tell me you get it when I stand up. We'll meet at the boxing
gym in Brooklyn or another spot after lunch and you can tell
me what you learned. I left you a present. It's next to me in
a brown bag.*

Flipping the note in the fireplace, Rob stands up. "I'll get there
before noon. You are a little ridiculous."

Fred walks out after buying some tobacco, rolling papers, and
matches.

MGL grabs the bag that was sitting next to Fred and heads out.
Peaking inside, he sees a tiny hearing aid that his glasses will easily
conceal.

With exercise being Rob's addiction, he walks five miles and
lands at the restaurant well before noon. The menu is huge, boast-
ing 50 different taco combinations. Voracious, Rob orders 10 tacos
and some guacamole.

Sipping a Coke next to an empty table for six, MGL feels his
mind buzzing. He can't pick stocks like Coop or sense emotion,
but he can see thoughts. That's the skill that helped him hustle on
the street.

The combination of sugar and caffeine works well for his gift.
Sauntering in, casually, is Fred with three agents. They look like
agents, down to the matching blue-collared shirts. Fred yells, "I'll
hold this table. Just get me three fish tacos and a water."

MGL, who hasn't really used his gift like this, seems relatively calm. He smiles a nonchalant glance at Fred. He reads Fred's
mind. "STOP SMILING, ASSHOLE!" Further irritating Fred,
MGL laughs.

Four stuffed trays land on the table and before Fred says thank
you, MGL is dialed in. All three men don't trust Fred.

Trying to be subtle, Fred asks the new guy, Newman,
"What's your take on Kastric?" Blocking out the rest of the
conversation, MGL zooms in on their thoughts. Bouncing
between each man is like playing a tennis match but at both
ends of the court. It's easier for him to focus on one person at

a time. There's a lot of information that is not said. Typing the takeaways into his phone:

- *Mob is feeding them info*
- *Kastric has an extensive list of 5% people across the globe*
- *Kastric might have info internationally on weapons, drugs, sex trafficking*
- *U.S. wants to cut a deal with him for info but unsure if he's for real*
- *Selling secrets has made him globally popular but widely hated*
- *Working on a 5% pill, selling DNA, and other sick lab experiments*
- *Currently in Boston, near universities, maybe meeting with hedge fund managers*

The four men continue to eat as MGL gets up and tosses out his food, including four tacos. His eyes, per usual, were larger than his stomach. He can feel Fred's irritation. Fred wants Rob to hang out longer to learn more.

Looking at the table, Fred notices MGL left his phone. "Excuse me, gentlemen. That man left his phone."

Grabbing the phone, Fred runs out the door. He chases down Rob, who unlocks his phone for Fred to read the notes. Promptly deleting them, Fred states, "So I have one more wish. Go home. Be safe. No need to meet later. Thanks."

MORE HELP

Briefing their senior ranking officer, Tal and Ari tell Maya everything they know, which is not much. She responds, "Work your contacts. Everyone is protecting that asshole! Between your new friends, one of them must know something. I'm not dealing with Trump. Head to the States, no trouble. Gather more info, we talk in a week."

While walking out of the facility, Ari picks up his burner phone.

Once again excusing himself, Fred heads to the bathroom as his phone buzzes. Unsure of the number, he answers anyway. "Hello. Who is this?"

"I'll give you a hint: I love a good falafel. My friend and I were told to visit the States. Any recommendations?"

With a smile on his face, "Man, you have no idea how happy I am to hear your voice. See you in Cambridge."

Before the line goes dead, Tal is buying tickets to Boston on his phone.

The Middle East doesn't need a man like Kastric to continue to spread secrets, treat the 5% like lab rats, and do God-knows-what-else to the highest bidder. Tal and Ari have continent-hopped for too long not to capture the scumbag.

Back at lunch, Fred is quizzed on what he knows about Kastric. Each time he answers a question he asks one. Trying to sneak out a little more intel. No one is really offering real info, but little by little they confirm what he read on MGL's phone. Building an image of what Kastric is doing in Boston slowly grows in his head.

Aside from recruiting at the universities, he's meeting with hedge fund guys. The movie in his head plays Kastric selling secrets, building an army, genetic testing people. What is this guy up to? So many angles.

As lunch ends, the only next steps are to talk to all sources and regroup in a week. Kastric is not to be killed; they want a meeting.

Afraid of being followed, Fred heads to the train station. Catching a train from New York to Boston seems like the best approach. His only thought is capture and kill. Kastric is probably heavily guarded, so hopefully Tal and Ari can help him out.

MOROCCO

Sleeping from the moment they sit in their seats to the moment they land, Natalie and Coop are ready for the next adventure.

While waiting to get off the plane, Coop turns on his phone and gets busy. Watching him work, Natalie comments, "Wow, you read reviews quickly. Glad we are staying near the beach. Three days?"

Coop, with a confused look, "Four days? I'm not sure what our next move is."

Natalie adds, "Three days is a good start. It will be nice to simply be. The past few weeks of chaos has allowed me zero time to think about what I need to do."

The ocean water, unlike Lake Michigan, is a deep blue. Following the coastline to the hotel, both Coop and Natalie gaze at the water. It's almost hypnotizing. The silence is welcomed until Coop asks, "What are you thinking about?"

Only making eye contact with the water, "How did I get here? I was working for an investment firm. I told them to drop Kastric's company, my boss dies, and here I am. It's just ridiculous. The oddest thing, the head partner was so phony about her death. He put on his fake face and pretended to be so sad, but I knew. It was only an act."

"What's his name?"

Natalie, shaking her head in disgust, "Matthew Benz. He must be connected to Kastric. Any large investment over a few million, he was usually the point person. The guy only cares about money."

Sensing a lot of hostility, "Alright, we'll pay him a visit. But first, beach time."

The Sofitel Hotel looks modern, open, and sparkling clean. The entire façade is white. Natalie comments, "This place is gorgeous. You are spending some coin."

Laughing, "I've paid double this to stay in New York per night, but this place is awesome."

Their suite has a small kitchen, an office area, a king bed, and a deck that overlooks the beach. The windows are open, and the perfect breeze seems fake. Sensing anxiety, Natalie puts her arm over Coop's shoulders. "Your old man will be okay, and we'll figure it out. Nothing to do today but relax."

Laughing, Coop adds, "We don't even have bathing suits."

Taking off her clothes, Natalie approaches Coop slowly and removes his clothes. "We can shop later."

Sex leads to a wonderful nap. Coop wakes up first and throws his clothes back on. Pulling out his phone, he shoots a name to Fred: Matthew Benz. He quickly deletes the message and picks up a guidebook.

With Natalie zonked out, Coop researches: shops, restaurants, and tickets back to the States.

WATCHED

While Shelly runs errands, Sam decides it's time to check in on Colt, Fred's FBI contact.

Working in the Chicago office, Fred knew Colt well. When Colt started, Fred helped train him. With serious trust issues, Colt was one of the only guys Fred could confide in. Sam has no idea if Colt is legit, but needing to protect Shelly pushes him to dial Colt.

"Hello, Colt. This is Sam."

Smiling over the phone, "So glad you called. We have been monitoring the area. No sighting of any mob or other activity in Chicago. Fred did remove your name from a list a while back. Doesn't mean you're safe, but it would be a stretch. Stay quiet the next few days. Call me if you run into any trouble. I'll keep an eye out for you."

Before Sam can say thank you, the line goes dead.

Sam's nerves settle, but not enough to keep him from punching and kicking his heavy bag. Working out the immense guilt he feels for stealing Coop's picks pushes him into a deep sweat. A deeper guilt sets in as he realizes he would know none of these moves if it wasn't for Coop.

No one wanted to spar with Coop. Although everyone loved him, he was intimidating. Muscles popping out, judo awards, jiu-jitsu trophies, and all the crazy weapons he kept in his room—who would want to fight with that? He promised to go easy on Sam. They started out boxing, then worked through all the weapons. The sudden-violence training was the worst—all elbows and kick moves left Sam bruised for weeks. Insisting it was important, Coop told him, "These are fake knives. Come on—one more round."

Once Sam finishes his workout, he decides to check out a jiu-jitsu studio. It's time to up his training.

Shelly, in the meantime, is also upping her game. She's training with Sam twice a week and really likes boxing. Once a week, she works out at a boxing gym. Pounding away her nerves has been an effective sleep aid. Slowly but surely, she's accepted looking over her shoulder. Knowing Sam is not in the 5% eases her fears.

BOSTON

Tal and Ari take the morning to sleep off some jet lag. They have one mission: capture and question Kastric. Sitting at lunch, Tal turns to Ari. "Does Kastric really have secrets?"

Without hesitation, "If he has Middle East secrets, he would be either protected or dead. No way he's flying around the world if he has some sort of special intel."

Without missing a beat, Fred sits down next to the Israelis. "Gentlemen, thanks for the text. I received a message from Coop. Matthew Benz. That was all I got. I did some research. I think that's why Kastric is here. Natalie worked for him. She was the one that suggested pulling their investment with Kastric's company."

Ari asks, "You check out Benz?"

With a smile, "Of course. He's a real piece of work. Loaded with a capital L. Ruthless businessman. Buys companies, tears them apart, sells them piece by piece. He invests in small pharma companies that make cheap drugs, and after his investment, they sell the same drugs at higher prices. The king of loopholes. He's known for having a team of global lawyers to cover his tracks."

Tal, usually silent around others, "We tail him. Leads us to Kastric."

With eyes on him, Fred nervously says, "That's the plan. Once we take care of Kastric, I need to disappear. U.S. doesn't want him dead."

Looking at an iPad, Fred adds, "Benz is leaving his house. Pay and meet me out front."

Fred's black Mustang looks and smells brand new. Ari, getting into the back, asks, "You just buy this?"

With a smile, "I borrowed it for the day. Fasten your seat belt." Handing Tal an iPad, "Navigate, big guy."

Other than the occasional directional order, the ride is quiet. Fred's hoping that Benz leads to Kastric. Once that happens, they will tail him and look for an opportunity to snatch him.

Ari, looking at the video, asks, "When and how did you tag the car?"

With a deceptive smile, "I don't know what you're talking about. I'm on vacation this week."

MOROCCO SUNSETS

Purple, pink, and orange colors fill the sky. The scenic view has decompressed Natalie. Picking at his dinner, Natalie can tell Coop is the opposite: anxious and nervous. Attempting to relax, Coop stares at the horizon. He can't let his guard down until Kastric is no longer a threat.

Sensing his emotions, "You need to find your dad. I get it. You want to make sure this is all behind you."

"I need to make this right. I can't relax until your life is safe. But I want you to stay here. Give me two weeks, and I'll come back for you."

Smiling, Natalie adds, "I know you're tough, but maybe you could use a little help."

Coop fires back, "I've been training for this my whole life. Despite my mom's begging to avoid this crap, she prepared me well. I have a few black belts, weapons training, and my mind is sharper than it's been in years. And only Sam can vouch for me, but I won two axe-throwing competitions. I can handle this."

Trying not to laugh, "You are ridiculous. You grew up training to be in a *Fast and Furious* film."

The aroma of fresh vegetables and slow-cooked lamb fills the air. Breathing in the spices interrupts the deep conversation.

Taking a sip of wine, Natalie adds, "This smells amazing. Maybe I could stay here for a while."

The food disappears quickly, as does the wine. This is the first time Coop's had a drink in weeks. His mind settles down. "Will you actually stay here?"

With a deceptive smile, "For you, anything." Looking at the coastline, "I used to take these great vacations every year after college. I took my parents on a trip one year. They had no idea how much money I was making until we reached the hotel in Hawaii. My dad turns to me, and before saying thank you, he tells me how proud he is of me."

Coop took a lot of trips with his mom. They would road trip during spring break and fly somewhere else during the winter. "Right before my mom got sick, we went to London. She always wanted to go there."

Holding hands under the table feels normal. As the liquor kicks in, Coop continues to relax. Natalie never imagined this adventure with Coop would happen. She sensed trouble on her end and compassion in his eyes, but the connection that's developing is unlike anything she's experienced before.

"I like you, Coop."

A big smile forms on Coop's face. "How are you so sweet and so gorgeous? It's a dangerous combination for me."

The dinner ends and a walk on the beach ensues. The moon's pale glow reflects off the water and lights up the white sand. Trying to be present, Coop rests his arm over Natalie. Feeling like he's in a relationship is something Coop has never experienced before. With a crazy upbringing, trusting anyone has always been a challenge. This seems easy, much different than his parents' fiery relationship.

ONE MORE TEAMMATE

The drive to the hotel is filled with a sea of colors. Spring in Boston is in full bloom—good thing MGL brought allergy meds. What pulled him to help Fred is a love of adrenaline and friendship. Not many people have a fairy godfather, but Rob does and it's Fred. There would be no nickname, Mister Good Life, without Fred.

Watching over Coop for all these years was easy. They were friends, and if anything, Coop's tips made MGL wealthier than he ever imagined.

Knowing Fred's love of the water, discrete location requirement, hotel with a free breakfast, and proximity to Mexican restaurants, the Lore must be his hotel. It checks all the boxes.

MGL checks into the hotel and heads right to the breakfast area. All these years knowing Fred, he's picked up on a few habits: workout in the morning, shower, and enjoy a stiff drink at night. While scanning the room, two men talk with Middle Eastern accents. Trying to play it cool, MGL reads their minds. Something about a crazy old man, already outside.

Following the two outside, he spots Fred in a sporty Audi. As the two men step inside, MGL yells, "Hey buddy!"

Fred waves him in. "Ari, Tal, this is Rob—aka MGL."

Shaking hands, "You can call me Rob. Nice to meet you."

Immediately Fred starts in, "What the fuck are you doing here?"

Sensing he can speak the truth, "None of your CIA buddies trust you. You've gone rogue. I thought you needed help. I had no idea the IDF was here."

Ari cuts in, "I like this guy. We have been tracking this guy, Matthew Benz. Your friend Fred somehow gets a new car every day. All we learned: Benz is a creep. Shady business deals, hookers, and we think today he sees Kastric."

While everyone gets situated, Fred turns on a radio. The fuzzy background noise clears up as he messes with some control buttons on his iPad; next up, video. Ari shakes his head, "You added cameras. No wonder no one trusts you. Are we being recorded, too?"

"Funny. We were getting nowhere. Today, I believe Kastric gets in the car, and we'll have audio and video. There also might be a bomb. I can neither confirm nor deny that."

Tal, usually quiet, "We can't just blow up two people because they suck. Can we?"

About four cars behind Benz, they watch a Town Car pull over and pick up two men. Fred has a smile ear-to-ear on his face. Sobriety really does help his powers. The door slams and conversation immediately flows. "Kastric, what the fuck are you doing? Tracking down five percent from the mob, selling secrets, what happened to running Tageo?"

"I'm diversifying. You wanted me, too, remember? Plus, the government thinks I know all this shit; they won't try and arrest or kill me."

Benz cuts right in, "I meant more alternative energy products or more supplements. Not messing with the mob and getting all crazy with five percent experimentation. You can't build an army with these people. Let's make money. Whatever happened to my old colleague? I can't believe you killed the wrong woman."

Fred whispers, "See? Cause."

Kastric's voice cuts back in, "I was never going to kill Natalie. I wanted her to get me my money back. And she did. She is five percent, but her skill is not so useful. I did get her stem cells, too.

We were going to do more tests in Italy, but she was saved. That motherfucker will die! I will find him, whoever he is."

Fred's heart is racing. The only good thing is that they have no idea who his son is and where they are. He could blow up that car and no one would really care. More chatting interrupts his thoughts.

Benz yells, "FOCUS! You had a booming business. This side hustle must end. I'm having trouble convincing my partners your company is stable. Other than our meeting, why are you stateside?"

Kastric, laughing, "I can make a fortune with a few more talented people. These mob assholes only sold me the rejects, but I know some of them are bright. And the others will be muscle."

Stopping the car, Fred stares at MGL, scrunched in the back seat. "They are going after Sam probably and you too. Head home and help him out. They don't know his new address but I'm sure with social media they will find out where he works, hobbies. I've been following his Instagram posts. He's working out at a jiu-jitsu club in River North. Don't call him. Be safe."

Without a word, MGL heads out of the car and crosses the street. He's already got a Lyft driver on the way.

Zeroing back in on the conversation, the three super friends are trying to figure out if Benz is bad or just sleazy.

"Don't you read, Kastric? The Israelis are way ahead of you on the research; give up the five percent. Focus on Tageo. You have less scrutiny there than here. I can't just convince the board to re-invest. Settle down, give me time, and it can be hundreds of millions for you."

Kastric responds, "I'll make that without you. I have a new partner."

While driving, Fred can't see the video, but Ari lets him know, "He's going to shoot Benz!" The loud bang stuns everyone. The driver shouts, "Oh MY GOD!"

Kastic barks out driving directions, "Calm down. You follow my orders, and you live."

Knowing that's not true, Fred interjects, "Do I blow up the car? He's going to kill the driver."

Ari, angry, "We save the driver's life. Follow him. He can't kill them until they are parked somewhere." Then asks, "His car bulletproof?"

"Yes. Best bet: T-bone. Can either of you tell me where he's going? Use a map, your super brains, or phone. This ends today."

BACK ON THE ROAD

Heading back to Italy, alone, Coop wants to learn what Dr. Lorenzo is up to. With a fake mustache, hat and sunglasses, Coop sits and waits at a coffee shop near the doctor's office. What is the leading researcher on stem cells doing with Kastric? The other thought buzzing around his head: Are Sam and his dad okay?

The good doctor walks by and Coop quickly joins him in stride. Without missing a beat, "Nice disguise. What can I do for you?"

"What are you doing with Kastric? Why stem cells?"

Taking a deep breath, "All the work we do is legitimate. He pays me for tests, samples, and storage. He also pays me to verify if people have five percent DNA. Before he tries to convince someone to sell us stem cells, he wants to make sure they are gifted. His new business is designer DNA. He's taking samples of five percent and selling it to people. Your friend, she is very keen with emotions. A parent who has a child with autism will pay for an injection that might help alter DNA. The science is currently iffy, but there's a chance it helps."

Walking past his office, the two continue to talk. Coop asks, "Why are you answering my questions?"

With no hesitation, "I'm not a bad guy. I'm a scientist. Your old President, Bush, didn't want to do this type of research. He set you guys back decades. I want to cure disease, help the sick. Who knows, maybe your stem cells could help someone with Parkinson's. The one thing about him, he's got people everywhere. Best you leave town. You should know, he has a partner."

Before he can read the doc's mind, "Oren!"

"Impressive guess. He's a crazy scientist. He's cutting guys open, while alive, testing the brain. He's sending me frozen brain tissue. You're going to need some luck."

Without a handshake or even a glance, the two separate and Coop heads back to the airport. Designer DNA, selling stem cells, and there's probably other work that Dr. Lorenzo doesn't know about it. And Oren, WTF? Was he always bad? Is that how he knew all about the tests? Was he working with Kastric before? What about the other two Israelis?

Contemplating his next few moves, Coop plans on visiting Sam, checking in on MGL, and then traveling out East. Maybe a trip to the Middle East. Lastly, back to Morocco to pick up Natalie.

Waking up alone is nothing new for Natalie; she just hoped Coop would be next to her, instead of a note.

Dear Natalie,

I miss you already. Stay here like we discussed. Have fun, see the sights, and I'm sure you'll do lots of reading. The last few days were amazing. I have never had days or nights that passionate, and I look forward to many more. The cash on the table has nothing to do with the sex =), for the record. The old man gave me a chunk. Better to use than your card.
Thinking of you,
Coop

INSURANCE

Driving around the block, Fred starts to speed up. "Buckle up, boys!"

Broken glass, smashed doors, a piercing noise, and smoke fill the air. Ari asks first, "All okay?"

The driver of the other car steps out first, dazed but okay. His bodyguard stumbles out of the car next, swearing in Fred's direction. "You fucking blind? What the fuck? I hope you have insurance." As he reaches for his gun, Tal smashes his elbow into the man's nose and opens the back door. Kastic, who chose not to wear a seat belt, is unconscious, possibly dead, head dangling on the seat. Tal picks him up and places him in the driver's seat.

As the driver tries to run away, Ari catches up to him, hands him some cash. "You overslept, missed work."

Fred, shaken but unharmed, checks for a pulse on Kastric. Nothing. He grabs Kastric's phone and tosses it to Ari. As they walk away, to be on the safe side, Fred detonates the bomb he left in the car.

As the BOOM sounds, Tal asks, "Did you have to do that?"

Fred, without missing a beat, "Yes."

Ari turns towards Fred, "Now what?"

"I have to disappear. You guys are good to go."

Tal shakes his head. "We actually wanted to question him. Capture, not kill."

Since Tal is not big on talking, his words weigh more. Fred, feeling no guilt, "Fuck you. In no world does that guy need to live."

Ari cuts in. "He has a partner. We need to find him. Some guy is helping him run tests on five percent. Crazy shit."

A little guilt creeps into Fred's head. "Sorry. Best you guys get out of here."

A few blocks away from their hotel, Tal and Ari hop out of the banged-up car. Before closing the door, Ari comments, "Good luck, Fred. We'll be around if you need us. We have your digits."

"You guys are my super friends. If I get a lead on Kastric's partner, I'll let you know."

Driving away, Fred starts to plan his next moves. How can he disappear but still watch out for Coop? Will the FBI and CIA ever figure out what he did?

Parking outside a lot with a car crusher, Fred tosses the mechanic a few hundred bucks. "I want to watch."

With a smile, "Whatever you're into, buddy."

REUNITING

When the plane lands in Chicago, Coop feels like he's home. The entire flight, Coop had odd dreams about his friends and Oren. While the plane taxis, Coop begins formulating his plan:

- *Find Sam & MGL*
- *Reach out to Fred*
- *Track down Oren*
- *Travel back to Natalie*

Hopping on the train, Coop heads to Wicker Park. Shelly lives somewhere around there, and Coop could use some ramen from Furious Spoon and a nap. With jet lag starting to settle in, Coop heads to a foot spa for a cheap massage and nap. After an hour massage/nap and some coffee, Coop's feeling great and senses Sam.

Heading farther west, he walks around Bucktown, letting intuition be his guide. Staring into a jiu-jitsu gym, Coop sees Sam rolling with a black belt. A smile forms on his face as Sam holds his own. Scanning the area for trouble, Coop sees no threats.

Catching Coop's eyes, Sam's face lights up; he runs out of the gym. With open arms, they squeeze each other as if they are long-lost brothers. "Man, I missed you! First MGL pops over to say hi to me yesterday, and now this. Even better."

Thinking that's odd, but ignoring the feeling, Coop soaks up the joy. "So MGL is good? Ramen?"

Heading for lunch, Coop can't get a word in edgewise as Sam's excitement leads to word-vomiting everything his buddy missed. "Shelly is the best. Really. Even with all this scary shit, she's been great. And MGL is now my friend. He checks on me every now and again. We grab a beer. He helped me get a new job, too. Making more cash. What about you?"

"I'm just happy to see you, Sam. I missed you. Going from everyday breakfast to radio silence was tough. Natalie is safe for the moment. I think Kastric is about to get arrested, and my next step is finding his partner. Have you noticed anything weird?"

Burrowing his eyebrows in deep thought, Sam comments, "Nothing out of the ordinary. I did get a call to see if I was a bone marrow match for a kid. I sent in a swab but never heard back."

Coop starts laughing. "You're fine. They are smart. If you get a call, let me know. I have to head out of town but needed to see you."

Sam looks confused, so Coop explains, "The mobsters are getting smart. There's a gene in your DNA for five percent. Some five percent folks don't know they have a gift. The mob first checks for the gene. If you test positive, then they test you in other ways. It's complicated but I think that means you are off their radar. If a company asks you for more DNA, tell them you're sick. Please. Trust me."

Another tight hug occurs as they head their separate ways. Sam adds, "Thanks for everything. Hooking me up with MGL and Shelly. I cannot believe you found me someone so amazing. And fighting skills. I had no idea what a bad ass you made me. I'm tossing around brown belts."

"Don't hurt anyone, tough guy. I'll see you soon. Tying up some loose ends." Before walking away, Coop gives Sam a phone and a hug.

NEW YORK NEW YORK

Trying to fly under the radar, Coop takes the train to New York. It also allows him time to research Dr. Oren Nashun. His work with the 5% is unparalleled. Universities from around the world consult with him on brain research. Why would he join Kastric? What happened when he was "captured?"

The first call in New York is to Fred's cell. No dice. Fred must've already gotten a new burner phone. Following Oren's advice, Coop gets some nicotine gum and drinks a coffee. His senses are on high alert, and even though he's confused who to trust, he calls Ari.

Ari, excited to hear Coop's voice, "You are safe! Kastric is dead. We are searching for his partner. And we are in the States."

Coop responds quickly, "Give me a hint."

"We will see how smart you are. My friend, it's a huge belt. In the city where dreams are made."

Coop, laughing, "Okay, Alicia Keys. See you shortly."

Without wasting any time, Coop googles the Orion hotel and walks east. With no weapon, no evidence, and no idea who's good, the plan is to tell the truth and read their minds.

Speedwalking, Coop reaches the hotel in 20 minutes. His heart is beating like he sprinted the entire way.

Sitting down on a bench outside the hotel, like they are working on their tans, are Ari and Tal. Ari speaks first. "Sit. I'll fill you in."

Cars and people zip by. The city that never sleeps is buzzing at 10 a.m. like work just got out. Nervous, Coop sits down.

"Fred still alive?"

"Yes. I'm going to give you the CliffsNotes version. Kastric shot Benz. Your dad blew up the car Kastric was in. He said he had to disappear. Glad the evil mad man is dead, but we just learned he has a partner."

Reading their minds, Coop can see they have no idea it's Oren. Currently, nowhere in their minds are any thoughts of Oren. This relieves Coop, but also makes him question their skills.

"It's Oren. Your buddy. Kastric and him are selling designer DNA. Trying to get ahead at work, here's some stem cells from a genius. Trying to make the Olympics, cells from someone with quick reaction time. The list goes on. Big money."

Tal, with his massive hands, makes a fist. "I knew we could not trust Oren. Makes me so mad."

Ari cuts him off. "That makes sense. Oren agreed to visit Kastric. He said, bring me to him. He wants to learn from me. That scumbag! Could be anywhere in the world."

With his mind still operating in high gear, Coop thinks the obvious. "You can call him or use his number and track him through your phone."

Tal, the tech savvy one, searches his phone. "You guys in the mood for some legit falafel?"

Coop, suddenly excited, "I have never been to Israel before. Let's head to the holy land!"

Smiling, Tal cuts in. "Michigan, silly. They have a large population of Chaldeans; they are Catholic Arabs. A lot of other Middle East folks live there too."

Trying to figure out where Oren is going next is the hard part. Ari pulls out a phone. "I have an idea." Scrolling down on Kastric's contacts, he sees Oren's number. "Tomorrow? Let's meet."

Before Coop can ask the question, Ari answers, "Fred gave us the phone."

The phone buzzes with a reply. "You still on the East Coast? Your goons did not find any good DNA for me yet. One more test from Chicago though. Just leaving Detroit."

Ari keeps it simple, "Yes. Central Park noon. Strawberry Fields?"

Oren responds, "K. See U tomorrow."

Questions swarm through Coop's mind. "You guys like the Beatles? What now? Can you just arrest him?"

Tal, unusually verbose, "We LOVE the Beatles."

With no suggestions, Coop takes over. The plan is simple. Disguise themselves and wait for Oren to get frustrated and walk away, then follow him. He's a scientist, not a spy, but it's not going to be easy. Searching for possible curve balls, Coop starts writing down notes. With all the stimulants running through his blood, the pen has trouble keeping up with his thoughts.

Ari, gazing at Coop's notes, comments, "We can grab him. Evidence would help, though. We need proof he's some evil scientist."

Not even two minutes later, a text interrupts their planning. Kastic's phone has a new message from Oren. "Meeting prospect in AZ lab. Sorry. Next week."

Grabbing the phone, Coop searches for "lab." Ari, impressed, peeks over Coop's shoulder.

"You found it! Time to book some flights."

While Ari books the tickets, Coop frantically dials MGL. "Don't go to Arizona."

"Coop, relax. It's legit. I'm helping out a sick kid."

"You might be helping out a kid, but they found something else in your DNA. Shit, I can't believe I never put it together. I just thought you were a lucky of son of a bitch. How did I miss it?"

Quickly responding, "I'm really good at sounding dumb. I'll get you evidence. You need a man on the inside. Even over the phone I can read your mind. See you there. Track me through the phone."

ARIZONA

Sitting on a plane usually leads to napping for Coop. Not today. Taking a few deep breaths, Coop tries to think positive thoughts. MGL is a smart guy. He made great money investing, but he's not a spy.

Sensing Coop's anxiety, Ari asks, "What's going on?"

Shaking his head, "How did I miss this? I've known this guy for years. I don't have a good feeling about this."

Placing his hand on Coop's shoulder, "We got you. We'll get some proof and take the scumbag back to Israel."

Immediately reading Coop's face, Ari adds, "You can trust us. Come on. We've been through some shit. I watched your old man blow up a fucking car."

Laughing hard, "That's my old man."

Tal removes his earbuds and adds, "We met MGL in New York. We got the entire story. This dude has been looking out for you. We're going to repay the favor."

Twice in Coop's life, he's been shocked: when his father left and when his father popped back into his life. Now, while the Boeing 747 descends, he's shocked for a third time. Meeting MGL seemed so random and amazing. Flashing back to that first beer, it felt so natural. Of course, Coop was a few drinks into the night, which dulls the mind. Holy shit—the first few meetings were always over drinks, even when they discussed business.

Staring into the aisle, "All this time I always liked him so much that I would give him these stock tips. Recently, I asked him to watch over Sam. Fuck. He was watching me. Ridiculous."

Ari chimes in. "Your dad basically saved his life. Got him off drugs and the streets. Helped him get his life together. And yeah, he kept that from you, but it all worked out. And it will all work out now."

Chewing on more nicotine gum and drinking a coffee, Coop focuses on Ari and Tal. The only sense he picks up: justice. They want Oren brought down. Both Tal and Ari feel conned. Oren was too smart for his own good.

Ari adds, "Ever since we parted, we've been studying this pyscho partner of Kastric's. These tests he's running are like something out of *Silence of the Lambs*. It's like shit Hitler would do, and we will not let that continue. I feel like I'm starting to talk like Fred."

Forcing a smile, Coop says, "Let's not blow up his car. I think jail will work better."

The hot air feels like a sauna. Thankful the rental car was underground and already cooled off, they step inside and start feeling better. Coop drives away like he's in a race car. The red Ford Explorer has more pickup than expected. Based on MGL's phone, he's staying forty minutes outside of Scottsdale. Without getting too close, Tal finds a motel about fifteen minutes off the highway.

UNDERGROUND

Lying on the beach in Costa Rica with a lemonade feels empty. Fred hasn't taken a vacation in years, and usually it's celebratory. When he told his CIA peers he needed time off, they were all for it. They felt he was a little too into Kastric. Covering his tracks isn't worrying him; it's figuring out the partner. The animal instinct to take care of his son continues to build, and he lets vengeance replace thinking.

The worry combined with sobriety has his mind playing movies over and over again. In all the clips, Coop lives, and that eases his mind. The guilt that he drank away for years runs deep. Memories of Coop's childhood flood his thoughts.

Although Emma denied Coop's mental prowess for years, Fred always knew his kid had a gift. At age 2, Coop spoke in complete sentences and remembered everything. Driving to a friend's house, he would remember where to turn, their address, and, most importantly, the snacks in their pantry. Danny's house was his favorite place to visit; they had Oreos and spicy tortilla chips.

Once Coop hit 5, all he wanted to do was box or hit baseballs. The moment Fred walked in from work, Coop would attack him with gloves on. Always anticipating the punches before Fred threw them, Coop was a natural fighter.

Pushing Coop to take judo was a little hard to watch. The first few tournaments were gut wrenching, as kids tossed around a scared, underweight toddler. By his third tournament, which was in Lincoln Park, Coop dominated. Fred joked that he had home-court advantage. Coop fought in two age groups, winning gold in both. That would also be the last time Fred saw him compete in person.

The first and only parent–teacher conference Fred attended was kindergarten. The teacher recommended skipping a grade. "He knows the answer to every question I ask. Sometimes, he raises his hand before I ask. And, more importantly, he's kind to friends."

Gazing into the ocean, Fred can't help but wonder: Is this vacation being kind to Coop? Should he be with him instead?

MARS BLACKMON

Waiting and waiting and waiting for a response from MGL terrifies Coop. They need to move out. Driving toward the medical facility takes no time. The parking lot is mostly vacant. Ari comments first. "They're gone. Probably locked his stuff up here, hence the phone signal."

Running out of the car, tears in his eyes, Coop races to the front door. A smiling woman greets Coop, but otherwise the office is empty. "Hi, sir. Can I help you?"

"Yes, my friend Rob told me he was helping a child today and to meet him here for a ride home."

"Your friend did a miracle today. If you could've seen the look on her parents' faces. It was beautiful. Anyway, he left a few hours ago. Sometimes they bring the donor to a bigger facility for fluids, or a hospital if it's worse. There's nothing in my system."

Walking back to the car, Coop feels like a failure. "He's gone."

Ari fires off, "Does he have a fancy watch?"

"Good call." Searching his app, he sees that MGL has ten thousand steps in, but the location is this clinic.

Sitting in silence, it hits Coop. With a smile, "It's got to be the shoes. MGL bought these shoes that track everything. Made me get a pair too. He's so competitive with running."

Two heads watch Coop as he finds the app, scrolls to MGL, and waits. "Searching for Runners" pops up, and then blinks with a location, which appears to be a hospital. With a deep exhalation, Coop fires up the car and starts driving.

With an inquisitive tone, Tal asks, "What's the plan now?"

Both Ari and Coop work on a plan in their heads before discussing. Coop suggests getting to the location first and then figuring out what to do. Driving with urgency, Coop flies down the highway.

As they pull into the parking lot, Ari fires off his plan. "Tal and I steal some scrubs. We are doctors. We ask the help desk for Dr. Oren Levi. You walk in and ask for MGL. One of us gets an answer. We free MGL first and then snatch Oren second. If rumors are true, he could have his head open. So mentally prepare for that."

Walking into the hospital, Coop senses MGL is alive, and somewhere within these walls. Ari and Tal quickly disappear among all the real doctors. The receptionist is new, and Coop knows she's overwhelmed. Greeting her with a smile helps ease her tension. "Hello. You are very busy. I am very nervous. My friend donated bone marrow and the facility on Rock Lane sent me here. Rob Snyder."

Clicking away on her computer, and trying to show empathy, "I believe he's in room 808. He's just recovering. Take those elevators."

While walking toward the elevators, Coop feels a buzz in his pocket. It's Kastric's phone, and the text is from Oren. "Just analyzed cells/brain of past drug user. Traces of LSD from twenty years. Maybe microdosing acts as catalyst. Testing theory in Chi Friday. Be back in NYC for the weekend."

Thoughtfully responding, "K. Take some protection."

Seconds later, "I got two goons. Thx for looking out."

Wasting no time, Coop calls Ari, "Meet me in room 808, elevator bank A."

Speedwalking to MGL's room, Coop's heart races. He hopes his guardian angel is okay, but the bandages around his head do not look like a good sign. Neither does the huge, drugged-up smile.

"Coop, buddy! How are you? I feel great! I met this little girl, saved her life!"

"He cut your head open? What the fuck? I'm going to kill that doctor."

Laughing, "Coop, he did a CAT scan. I stood up too soon after the procedure and hit my head." As if he's a doctor, Coop scans his friend. He sees the ice pack on the back of his head and exhales.

Ari and Tal walk in as Dr. Coop decides MGL is okay. "I got a text from Oren. We need to head to Chicago. Apparently, they found LSD from years ago in Rob. Oren now wants to test whether microdosing LSD will cause DNA/brain changes in five percent prospects. It may unlock their powers."

Tal asks, "Why Chicago?"

"Simple: He has prospects there. One is my friend. He's got two guards with him."

Still loopy, MGL cuts in. "We can take my plane!"

"You can barely talk. How are you going to fly us almost four hours to Chicago?"

Tal cuts in, "I was a pilot in the IDF, and Ari has his pilot's license."

While they solidify their plans, a doctor walks in. "Gentlemen. If your friend can pass this exam, he's free to go. He should not operate any heavy machinery for four to six hours. He does not have a concussion, but he did hit his head pretty hard."

As the doctor leaves, MGL collects his belongings and asks, "How did you find me?"

Coop, pointing at his feet, "It's gotta be the shoes."

TOUGH FRIENDS

Shelly and Sam are enjoying a quiet dinner in the kitchen. Sam's anxiety levels have finally dropped to normal. Life feels comfortable again, and then his phone rings—the burner phone Coop gave him.

Shelly waits for dialogue; all she gets is Sam saying, "Okay, okay. Will do."

Before she can ask a million questions, Sam says, "I need you to spend a few nights with a friend. All should be fine, but this guy is coming to town looking for me. Coop and his team are going to help me. I'll be okay."

Because she's the most understanding person on the planet, Shelly tells Sam exactly what he needs to hear: reassurance. "You will be fine. I love you. You should maybe join your grappling buddies for drinks tonight and do a double class. Lots of friends there to help you."

A few text messages later, Shelly has plans. Her friend Gail, who complains that Shelly has no time for her, is excited for a girls' night. "Gail is super pumped."

With a smile, "Of course she is. She's probably sick of going to the movies with us."

Packing up in minutes, Shelly fights off her desire to fight with Sam. "This is hard. I don't want to leave you, but I know it's for the best. I love you." With a tight hug and long kiss, Shelly heads to her friend's house. Feeling guilty that she's leaving, Shelly gives Sam one more kiss.

With both of his hands cupping her pretty face, "Shelly, I promise. I'll be fine. Coop will be with me, and my new friends from the gym can be very intimidating."

With a tight hug, "I know. Especially Jasper. That guy looks like a Marvel superhero."

Laughing, "He does. Now have fun. I'll text you." As Shelly leaves, Sam searches the apartment.

Shuffling through his "Coop drawer," he pulls out a Kubotan key ring. With a smile, he remembers the day Coop got them in the mail. He was like a kid at Christmas. With excitement overflowing, he spent two weeks showing Sam how to use this little weapon. Digging deeper, he finds the collapsible bow, another Coop favorite. They practiced with a foam version for weeks while Coop waited for the real ones to come in the mail. The weapon grows from the size of a pen to about three feet.

With a few weapons in his pocket, Sam heads out to meet friends. His phone buzzes. "Hello?"

"Hey. They're coming in from AZ; you probably won't hear from anyone till tomorrow. We'll be in and ready to help. Don't sweat it. It's going to be some medical angle hook."

Feeling a little less stressed, "Thanks. We'll get them. Found the bow and Kubotan."

Laughing, "Man, you don't need me. Those two weeks in college, I was ridiculous. Why did you ever stay friends with me?"

"I wanted to be a ninja like you."

The one thought that keeps popping into his mind: Why did he steal the picks? If he'd just left them alone, none of this would have happened. Raising money to get Coop a bar was his only goal.

Walking into Jasper's condo, Sam suddenly doubts the toughness in the room. "You guys are watching *Love, Actually*?"

ONE MORE TEST

Following MGL's directions, Tal and Ari land the plane like old pros. Coop comments first, "I'm not going to lie, I was a little worried with you two flying. Not that I don't have the utmost respect for you guys; but flying some dude's plane had to be a little nerve racking."

Tal, with a grin, "Have some faith. I spent years flying planes. I don't like helicopters, so I'm glad this was a plane."

Instead of renting hotel rooms, the group heads to Sam's place. Oren flew domestic; there's no way he's out of the airport yet.

Coop calls Sam. "Yo, we are here. Heading to your place. Cool if we all crash there?"

Letting out a yawn, "Of course. I'm at Watering Hose. It's about two blocks west on Milwaukee from my place."

Quickly agreeing to a drink and then rest, the crew heads to the bar. The only plan: Sam will meet Oren and then the others will show up. Coop tries to figure out what else could happen. He only has a few guys protecting him; it should be fine, but he's unsure.

Sensing Coop's anxiety, Ari comments, "Oren is a scientist. He has no gun. Maybe two bodyguards who are more like helpers. Trust me. Get some sleep."

Seven in the morning hits quickly and everyone is up but MGL. Taking his spot back in the kitchen, Coop starts cooking. The smell of fried eggs and pancakes fills the apartment in a fog. "How do you not have maple syrup?"

Defensive, "Um, we don't make pancakes. Did you just zest that lemon?"

Coop answers, "Of course. It adds great flavor to my flapjacks. And I guess honey works."

Eating breakfast and watching sports highlights feels like old times. Finally, MGL pops out of the guest room. "Man, my head is still killing me. Do I have a bump?"

Sam answers, "That's not a bump, that's an egg. Be careful, Coop might cook that."

Grabbing frozen peas from the freezer, MGL sits on the couch and lies back on the peas. "You think he clipped out some of my brain?"

Half kidding, Coop answers, "Probably. Can you read my mind?"

"Yes. And it's doubtful the Cubs will win the World Series. But for your sake, I hope they do."

A ringing phone interrupts the shenanigans. Sam puts his cell on speaker phone. "Hello."

"Hello, Sam. It's Dr. Smith. It turns out that even though you are not a match, I might have a research project for you. Interested in making five hundred dollars for a study?"

Playing along, "Sounds good to me. Nothing that will kill me, right?"

"Don't be silly. It's called microdosing. Sounds like we are getting you high, but not at all. I have a video I'm emailing you now. Watch it and call me back. I'm here until Friday afternoon."

Sam, hesitating for a moment, "Ah, this sounds crazy. I like crazy. Count me in. I'll watch the video and if it spooks me, I'll email you."

Oren responds warmly, "Of course. There is no pressure. I have a few other options. If it's too freaky for you, don't worry about it."

Ari and Tal are shaking their heads. He's using reverse psychology. They've heard this before from him.

"When and where, Doc?"

"Can you work half a day tomorrow? One-thirty? I have an office rented out in Lincoln Park."

With the nervous jitters starting to set in, Sam agrees and hangs up.

Hovering over Sam's laptop, he reads the email out loud. Oren wants to give him a small dose of LSD and see how that affects critical thinking. The dose will not be enough to induce a trip, but might alter his mind in other ways, increasing creativity, speeding up or slowing down aptitude, and several glasses of water will push everything out of his system.

Driving by the location, nothing stands out. It looks like an old medical office. Across from the office is a 24/7 taco joint. Coop starts barking out orders, "Starting at six a.m., Tal and MGL will take the first shift, watching out for Oren. Three hours later, Ari and I are on watch, and then we all meet there at noon."

Ari agrees first, "That sounds doable."

Coop yells to Sam, "Stop the car! Reverse slowly."

Shelly's white Camry slowly backs up. Sam kills the lights and they all stare at Oren hopping out of a car with two large men dragging in equipment. Coop asks, "Do we jump them? Get this over with? This seems too easy"

The two soldiers survey the scene before answering. Ari breaks the silence, "There's not a lot of people around. Tal can take the back entrance. I didn't see guns but I'm sure they have them. Tal?"

Tal looking anxious, "We take him tonight."

LONELY BEACH

Putting down her third book of the week, Natalie feels antsy. The relaxing days, kind people, and breathtaking sunsets are amazing, but with no one to share them with, Natalie packs.

Beyoncé's old song "Single Ladies" is blaring from the pool speakers, sneaking into Natalie's room. The song takes her back to her last real boyfriend, Bobby. It's been two years since they broke up, and a song—or flavor, like mocha almond fudge—will bring back memories. Never one to date bad boys, Natalie always had sweet and caring boyfriends. Bobby was the most thoughtful. He didn't have Coop's looks or sense of humor, but the man could dance. For some odd reason, he memorized the "Single Ladies" dance from the video, and that's how Natalie noticed him.

The biggest difference between Bobby and Coop, aside from Coop being a better kisser, is the protector gene. Bobby wanted to take care of her financially, but not emotionally or physically. On New Year's Eve, with no cabs in sight, he said, "You live four blocks from here. Call me when you get home." Coop wouldn't let that happen unless it was noon on a sunny day.

While being driven to the airport, fear creeps into her mind. What if Coop is mad she came? What if he's in trouble? Why hasn't he emailed or called? Something is not right. Finally calming down, she circles back to the protector role. Coop is staying away so no one can track her down. It's chivalry, but it's time to help him. He would've never been in this deep if it weren't for her.

Buying a fourth book at the airport, Natale senses anger. The man that tested her at Kastric's house is standing behind her. Reacting like a trained fighter, Natalie jams the binding into the man's temple and follows up with a quick elbow to the chin. Taking a page out of Coop's book, she grabs his wallet and, as he falls to the ground, screams, "THIS MAN JUST FAINTED! PLEASE CALL HELP!"

Noticing no cameras, Natalie adds a quick kick to his head before speedwalking to her flight. Thoughts flood through her mind. Maybe he's not bad. Maybe he was angry about something other than her. Wearing a big hat, sunglasses, and coat, it would be hard for him to know it was her.

Cleaning and flushing the blood off her shoes, Natalie peeks at his ID. Carmen Bardah, same last name as Kastric. He must've been in Italy and was trying to find her and Coop. Suddenly, she feels better about kicking him in the head. After tossing his belongings in the trash, Natalie nervously walks to her gate.

Shaking like a leaf, Natalie boards the plane and immediately asks for a drink. Turning on relaxing sounds, Natalie practices box breathing and slowly falls asleep.

TEXTING

Kastric's phone starts to blow up. Coop reads it to the guys while they watch Oren. "UR cousin was taken to hospital. Passed out. Found bruise on head and chin. Might've been attack. No one saw a thing. Some lady yelled for help. Moroccan airport."

Coop writes back, "Room number, hospital, name under? Why Morocco?"

Ari asks, "Morocco airport?"

With a laugh, Coop responds, "Natalie has turned into one tough girl. She's coming here. We were there."

The phone buzzes again. "Carmen. Escaping? He bought home there. Benz is dead. Another charred body was w/ him. Not sure who it was."

"Thx. Check on Carmen. Question him. Escaping?"

"Done. He said he was out after the last test."

Tal cuts the silence. "Oren is done loading. It's going to take them hours to set up. Let's do this. They look tired, too. I'll text Fred to check on Carmen."

Stroking his chin, Coop suggests, "Instead of Tal taking the back, you two go together through the front. He'll know something is up if you guys are not together. I'll take the back with Sam. MGL, you stay across the street. You can call the cops if this goes sideways."

Out of nowhere, Coop hands Sam a bat and takes one for him-self. Tal and Ari have guns and handcuffs. Ari asks, "Can we keep him alive? We want to question him. My boss said if the U.S. wants him, that's fine. He just has to get locked up. Between us, if they want him here, I think it's safer for everyone."

Subtly walking towards the entrance, the group tries not to draw any attention. Sam runs around the back. His heart races as if it's going to pop out of his chest. Breathing, self-talk, nothing seems to bring it down. Visualizing different punch and kick com-binations starts to settle him down.

Instead of worrying about the two guards, Coop wonders if he can trust Ari and Tal. His gut and heart say yes. And the few times he read their minds, it's always on the right side of the force.

The door to the lab is wide open. Coop sees Ari and Tal walk right in. Oren, surprised, starts running his mouth. "Hey guys! How did you find me? Been tailing me for a while? What can I do for you?"

Dismissing the guards, they head out front. Realizing they are just movers, Coop waves. "Hi, guys. You no longer work for Oren." He hands them a few bills and they smile.

Without a fuss, which is slightly surprising, they hop in a car and leave. Coop walks around back. His smile eases Sam's nerves. "Come in. It's just us and Oren."

Before they reach the front, a car zips into the lot, tires screech-ing. Holding a finger to his lip, Coop hushes Sam. Whispering, "There's going to be three of them. Use the bat on the legs first, then head."

Sneaking behind a post, they watch three men get out of the car and head to the trunk. While the goons are gathering weapons, Coop and Sam attack.

Without thinking, Sam takes out the first guy with a kick to the leg and a smack across the chin. He swings at the next guy's ribs, and as the giant of a man doubles over in pain, Sam cracks him in the head. Coop has his guy on the ground, Applying pres-sure to his arm, "Anyone else with you?"

"Just the doctor."

The adrenaline is starting to wind down for Sam. Turning to Coop, "What did we just do?"

"We helped the good guys. Head inside and see if they need help." Coop ties up the guys and tosses them in their own SUV, struggling a bit with the giant, who's heavy and still unconscious.

Attempting to talk his way out, Oren rants, "This is science. If the stem cell injections improve cognition, this will help millions of people. If we unlock improved brain function, we'll be actual heroes. Sure, Kastric is a piece of shit. But his ideas, lists, and connections made so much possible. What if I turn him in?"

Everyone laughs. Oren grows more frustrated. "What about the mob? I know things."

Siren noise and lights blast through the window and Ari cuts in, "Federal agents are outside. Good luck in prison."

Surprised, Oren shouts, "You aren't taking me home?"

With a smile, "I'll let the federal agents sort that out."

Walking outside, Coop turns to Ari. "Was that too easy?"

Ari answering, "We've been chasing Kastric for two years. This has not been easy! I lost two men and I thought Oren was a friend."

CLEANUP

Sitting at the beach was getting old fast for Fred. If he only knew Coop was okay, it would be much easier to relax.

A text message interrupts Fred's boredom. "Head to Morocco. Carmen Bardha. Cousin of Kastric's was seen there. He's at the local hospital. B safe. Henchmen also checking on him."

Smiling, Fred responds, "Finally. On it. Coop okay?"

"Yup. We think Carmen was escaping."

Surprisingly, there are direct flights, but only one per day. The only flight for the day leaves in two hours and has only first-class tickets. Good thing Fred's corporate card still works.

While buying all the snacks he can find at the airport shop, Fred has a vision. Three men standing outside a hospital room. His methodical mind builds a plan: Purchase scrubs, surgical mask, stethoscope, and nonslip shoes. For some reason, doctors in hospitals always wear rubber-soled shoes. The rest of the plan is simple: Ask for Carmen, walk past the bad guys, ask them to get some food for Carmen, and sneak him out. While taking his seat, Fred talks to himself. "Might even work."

The life of luxury in first class eases Fred's angst. After a long nap, the landing gear goes down, and he's ready for coffee and some nicotine gum.

REUNITED

Coop and Sam disappear before the investigators arrive. MGL sticks around, he gives his statement, and a medical examiner checks him over. He feels like a piece of meat as the doctor pokes and prods him. "Robert, can I check you out tomorrow at Northwestern Medical Center? I want to run a CT and make sure he didn't put a chip in you."

"That would be great. I hit my head hard, so there might just be a lot of swelling." The doctor hands him a card and walks away.

Ari and Tal are on a call speaking Hebrew. Their commanding officer, Yossi, is completely shocked that Oren has been working with Kastric. In the background they can hear Oren protesting, "I'm a doctor! This is research!"

The usually quiet neighborhood is buzzing like it's Friday night. People are on their balconies gawking at the mix of cop cars and military vehicles.

The long walk to Sam's house is therapeutic. "Coop, I can't believe this. Please tell me this would've happened even if I hadn't stolen your picks."

Laughing, "This is crazy. I spent my whole life trying to hide this side. Sure, I prepared for some of this but never, ever, did I think I would use duct tape like that. The fight training came in handy. It's crazy."

Sam's phone rings. Looking at his phone, debating whether to answer, Coop nods yes. "Hi Sam. Are you with Coop?"

Even though they only met briefly, Sam knows who it is right away, "Sure, Natalie. Glad you're okay. I'll hand Coop the phone."

On with Coop, Natalie says, "I know, I know I was supposed to stay away. I just couldn't. I like you, Coop. And I thought you would be proud—I called Sam's phone, not yours."

"I like you, too."

Running to the landline, Sam calls Shelly. "Come home! P.S. We have guests." The only words Shelly utters: "I love you, Sam."

UPDATES

Fred is enjoying Morocco. His game of disguise was for nothing. Carmen was in good health and left the hospital a day before Fred arrived. Being suave, Fred got his address. Carmen is retired, not dead. His cousin paid him handsomely and never let on about the more deplorable work Oren was doing. Without worrying about Coop, Fred has taken an extended vacation.

MGL is healing nicely. There was, in fact, a chip implanted in him. It was a tracking device—at least that's what the doctor told him. He's recovering peacefully on his boat.

Ari and Tal's long mission finally has ended. They are back in Israel enjoying the beautiful beaches—and the much-needed rest.

Sam and Shelly are engaged! The wedding will take place in late fall, with Coop as the best man.

Coop is renting a house in Logan Square. Natalie is looking for a place in Chicago and living with Coop until she finds one, which might be never. They started an investment office with MGL and are currently investing in bio-medical research. Legitimate firms only.